We climb down into the canyon. I am able to climb much faster now. I have learned by watching and imitating Wolf. My hiking boots are comfortable on my feet, as if they belong there.

At the bottom we rest on a rock. "Remember the time you told me I have sad eyes?" I say.

"I remember."

"It's because my father's dead."

Wolf looks at me, shakes his head slowly, and says, "We have a lot in common, Tiger . . . because mine is dying."

Later, when it is time to leave the canyon, I say, "I didn't make you laugh today."

And Wolf says, "I didn't feel like laughing." I ride home feeling very sad. I wish I could talk to my mother. But when I get back she is sound asleep again, the shades in her room pulled down, making it as dark as night. Sometimes I feel she has vanished from my life. And I miss her.

OTHER BOOKS BY JUDY BLUME YOU WILL ENJOY

THE PAIN AND THE GREAT ONE

THE ONE IN THE MIDDLE IS THE GREEN KANGAROO

FRECKLE JUICE

BLUBBER

IGGIE'S HOUSE

STARRING SALLY J. FREEDMAN AS HERSELF

ARE YOU THERE GOD? IT'S ME, MARGARET.

IT'S NOT THE END OF THE WORLD

DEENIE

JUST AS LONG AS WE'RE TOGETHER

HERE'S TO YOU, RACHEL ROBINSON

THEN AGAIN, MAYBE I WON'T

Tiger Eyes

Judy Blume

Published by
Laurel-Leaf
an imprint of
Random House Children's Books
a division of Random House, Inc.
New York

Visit us on the Web! www.randomhouse.com/teens

Educators and librarians, for a variety of teaching tools,
visit us at www.randomhouse.com/teachers

ISBN: 0-440-98469-6

Reprinted by arrangement with Macmillan Publishing Company,
on behalf of Bradbury Press

Printed in the United States of America

One Previous Edition
First Laurel-Leaf Edition October 1991
New Laurel-Leaf Edition April 2005

50 49

OPM

For George

contigo la vida es una buena aventura

ONE

It is the morning of the funeral and I am tearing my room apart, trying to find the right kind of shoes to wear. But all I come up with are my Adidas, which have holes in the toes, and a pair of flip-flops. I can't find my clogs anywhere. I think I packed them away with my winter clothes in a box in the attic. My mother is growing more impatient by the second and tells me to borrow a pair of her shoes. I look in her closet and choose a pair with three-inch heels and ankle straps.

I almost trip going down the outside stairs. My little brother, Jason, says, "Watch it, stupid." But he says it very quietly, almost in a whisper.

Mom puts her arm around my shoulder. "Be careful, Davey."

At the cemetery people are fanning themselves. We are in the midst of the longest heat wave Atlantic City has seen in twenty-five years. It is 96 degrees at ten. I think about how good it would feel to walk along the beach, in the wet sand, with the ocean lapping at my feet. Two days ago I'd stayed in the water so long my fingers and toes had wrinkled and Hugh had called me Pruney.

Hugh.

I see him as we walk through the cemetery to the gravesite. He is standing off to one side, by himself, cracking his knuckles, the way he does when he's thinking hard. His hair is so sun-bleached it looks almost white. Maybe I notice because it is parted on the side and carefully brushed, instead of hanging in his face, the way it usually does. Our eyes meet, but we don't speak. I bite my lower lip so hard I taste blood.

At the grave, I stand on one side of my mother and Jason stands on the other. I feel the sweat trickling down inside my blouse, making a little pool in my bra.

My aunt and uncle, who flew in from New Mexico last night, stand behind me. I have seen them only one other time in my life, when my grandmother died. But I was only five then and wasn't allowed to go to her funeral. I remember how I'd cried that morning, not because my grandmother had died, but because I wanted to ride in the shiny black car with the rest of the family, instead of staying at home with a neighbor, who tried to feed me an apricot jelly sandwich.

This time I haven't cried at all.

Now I hear my aunt making small gasping sounds, then blowing her nose. I hear my uncle whispering to her but I can't make out his words.

I feel their breath on the back of my neck and move closer to my mother.

Jason clings to Mom's hand and keeps glancing at her, then at me. My mother looks straight ahead. She doesn't even wipe away the tears that are rolling down her cheeks.

I've never felt so alone in my life.

I shift from one foot to the other because my mother's shoes are too tight and my feet hurt. I concentrate on the pain, and the blisters that are forming on my little toes, because that way I don't have to think about the coffin that is being lowered into the ground. Or that my father's body is inside it.

TWO

The heat wave breaks that night and the next day, when my best friend, Lenaya, comes to visit, it is still raining. She sits on the edge of my bed and piles up the newspapers that are scattered all around.

"Hi," she says. "How are you?" Her voice sounds shrill, not at all like her usual voice.

"I'm okay," I answer, not able to look directly at her.

"I'm sorry about your father."

I nod, afraid that if I try to speak I will break down and cry.

"It was a real shock."

I nod again.

"We were in Baltimore, so we didn't know until my uncle read it in the paper. He called to tell us. But by then there was no way we could get back in time for the funeral."

I felt myself drifting off, hearing only a few more words. I feel very far away, as if nothing that is happening is real.

On the day that we met, Lenaya gave me a picture of a dissected female frog. She'd drawn it herself, with colored pencils. Every organ was carefully labeled. Heart, stomach, lungs, ovaries. I still have the picture somewhere. In my bottom drawer, I think. That was in eighth grade.

Lenaya is six feet one, skinny and black. Everyone assumes she must be great at basketball, but the truth is, she hates the game. She'd rather do an experiment with her chemistry set or read a book on genetics.

My father played basketball when he was in high school. He made the All State team twice. He could have had a college scholarship but he and my mother got married instead. And six and a half months later I was born.

"Davey . . . are you awake?" Lenaya asks, bringing me back from my thoughts.

"Yes."

"Why don't you get out of bed and get dressed . . . it's after twelve."

"I don't feel like getting up. I'm tired. Besides, I've got blisters on my feet."

"Your aunt says you haven't been out of bed since the funeral."

"That's not true. I get up to go to the bathroom." I shift my position and as I do my cat, Minka, who has been asleep next to my leg, stretches, yawns and begins to lick herself. I stroke her under the chin until she settles down again. "Did you read the story in the paper?" I ask Lenaya.

"Yes," she says.

"Which one?"

"I don't remember."

I rummage through the pile of papers Lenaya had stacked a few minutes earlier, choose one, hold it up, and read the headline out loud. ADAM WEXLER, 34, SHOT AND KILLED. I show the article to Lenaya. "It made the front page," I say, tapping the paper with the back of my hand. "It's a nice picture of him, don't you think?" I don't wait for her to answer. "I took it myself . . . in June . . . in front of the store. He's shading his eyes from the sun but other than that he looks good, doesn't he?"

"Yes," Lenaya says, softly.

I put down that paper and pick up another. ADAM WEXLER, LOCAL MAN, MURDERED. I glance at Lenaya. Her head is bent and she is fiddling with her belt. I read from the paper.

> *"Adam Wexler was shot in the chest and killed Tuesday evening during a robbery in his 7-Eleven store on Virginia Avenue, Atlantic City. The unknown assailant or assailants escaped with fifty dollars in cash. Mr. Wexler, a 1964 graduate of Atlantic City High School, is survived by his wife, Gwendolyn; a daughter, Davis, 15; and a son, Jason, 7."*

I fold up the paper and toss it to the end of my bed.

"Do you think it's a good idea to keep reading about it?" Lenaya asks.

"Why not? Everyone says you have to face the facts. So I'm facing them." Newspapers are very big on facts, I think. But not on feelings. Nobody writes about how it *feels* when your father is murdered.

"In lieu of flowers the family has asked that contributions be sent to the American Heart Fund." I recite this for Lenaya, while I stare at the ceiling. I wonder why my mother has selected the Heart Fund, unless it is because my father was shot in the chest. Four times. Four times by an unknown assailant or assailants.

My aunt pokes her head into my room and says, "Lunch time, girls."

"I'm not hungry," I tell her.

"It's just soup and sandwiches," she says. "Lenaya . . . would you like to stay for lunch?"

"Sure," Lenaya says. "Thanks."

"I don't want anything," I say.

"You've got to eat, Davey. At a time like this it's important to keep up your strength. I'll fix you a tray. You and Lenaya can eat in your room. How about that?"

I nod. It is easier than arguing.

When she is gone I turn to Lenaya and say, "Her real name is Elizabeth but everyone calls her Bitsy. Isn't that a dumb name for a forty-seven-year-old woman? She's my father's sister.

I mean *was*. That's the way you put it when somebody dies, isn't it? You say *was*."

"I guess," Lenaya says.

"She's from New Mexico."

"I know. She seems nice."

"My uncle, Walter, is a physicist at the Lab in Los Alamos. That's where the first atom bomb was built."

"I know," Lenaya says again. "I was talking to him before, while you were asleep. I can't wait to take physics, but I think you have to be a junior."

Bitsy carries a lunch tray to my room. Lipton Country Vegetable soup, tuna fish sandwiches and iced tea, with lemon slices floating on top.

I watch as Lenaya begins to eat.

I take a sip of iced tea. Then I try a bite of tuna fish sandwich. I chew and chew until I feel myself gagging. I jump off the bed and race down the hall to the bathroom, where I spit the food into the toilet.

But this time I don't throw up.

THREE

On the night that my father was killed, after the police and the neighbors had left, Jason and I got into bed with Mom. We'd left a light on in every room. The house was very quiet and I thought about how strange it is that sometimes quiet can be comforting, while other times, it becomes frightening.

"What's it like to be dead?" Jason asked Mom.

"Peaceful," Mom told him.

"How do you know?" Jason said.

"I don't really," Mom said. "But it's what I believe."

"Suppose they come back?" Jason asked.

"Who?" Mom said.

"The guys who shot Daddy. Suppose they come back and shoot us, too?"

"They won't," Mom said.

"How do you know?" Jason asked.

"I just do, that's all," Mom said.

"Do you think it hurt?" Jason said.

"What?" Mom asked.

"When Daddy got shot. Do you think it hurt him?"

"No," Mom said. "I think it happened so fast he didn't feel a thing."

"That's good," Jason said. "Isn't that good?"

"Yes," Mom said, "that's good. Now let's try to get some sleep, okay?"

"Okay," Jason said, yawning, as he snuggled up against Mom and closed his eyes.

Mom looked at me. I didn't say a word. I couldn't. I reached for her hand and held it tightly. I rested my head on her shoulder.

FOUR

Walter and Bitsy stay with us for ten days and Bitsy offers to stay longer, to help my mother. But Mom says, "No, you've done enough already."

"There's no such thing as enough," Bitsy says. "We're family. Maybe we haven't seen much of each other over the years . . ." Her voice trails off.

"We kept planning a trip to New Mexico," Mom says, "but somehow . . ." She shakes her head. Neither one of them seems able to finish a sentence.

"Come with us now," Bitsy says. "The change would do you good."

"I can't," Mom says. "I've got to pick up the pieces by myself."

"All right . . . but we don't want you to worry about money, Gwen. We can help. We *want* to help . . . until you get back on your feet."

My mother presses her lips together and shakes her head again. "I think we can manage."

Bitsy gets up from the table and walks into the kitchen where she pours herself a third cup of coffee. I am standing by the stove, stirring honey into a cup of tea that I am not going to drink.

"I remember when he was born," Bitsy says. "He was such an adorable baby." At first I think she is talking about Jason. But when she says, "Always drawing . . . right from the beginning . . . and such a good student . . . such a fine athlete . . ." I realize that she means my father. "I still can't believe it . . ." Bitsy continues, her voice breaking.

I don't want her to cry. Not now. She takes a few deep breaths, blows her nose and the moment passes. She carries her coffee cup back to the dining area and sits down again. "No will, no insurance, no savings," she says to Mom. "What were you living on, anyway . . . love?"

"More or less," my mother answers.

Bitsy sighs. "Adam always was a dreamer."

"Yes," Mom says. "That's one of the reasons I loved him."

But we're all dreamers, I think. If you don't have dreams, what do you have?

Later, as Bitsy and Walter kiss each of us goodbye, Bitsy says, "We have a big house . . . and you'll always be welcome."

"We're only as far away as the phone," Walter adds.

"Thank you," Mom says. "I'm glad you were here. You were a real help."

I have mixed feelings when Walter and Bitsy leave. It's good to be by ourselves again. Just us.

Just the family. But it's also a reminder that my father isn't here anymore. That he won't be back. That from now on it will be *only* the three of us.

At night, I lie in my bed, frightened. I hear noises I've never heard before. With Bitsy and Walter sleeping on the sofa, in the living room, I wasn't so scared. None of us was. Now it's back to a light on in every room and Jason creeping into Mom's bed in the middle of the night.

I feel like going into Mom's room, too. With the three of us close together I don't feel so alone. *But I'm fifteen,* I keep reminding myself. *I can't sleep in my mother's bed forever.*

The worst times are when I start to think about the brown paper bag on my closet shelf. Then my heart beats very fast and I have trouble breathing. So I squeeze my eyes shut to erase the picture in my mind.

We live above the store and I listen for footsteps on the outside stairs. I'll have plenty of warning if anyone tries to get up here, I tell myself, touching the breadknife that I've hidden under my pillow.

And I'm not the only one who's prepared. My mother keeps the gun under her bed. She doesn't know that I know. But I do. I've seen her holding it. It's loaded. She's ready to use it, if she has to.

Not like Dad.

He kept the gun in the store, on a shelf right

under the cash register. But it wasn't loaded. He was afraid Jason would get hold of it or something. So the bullets were in a locked drawer and only my father had the key. We'd been robbed two other times, but the second time my father waved the gun at the guy and he took off with just a six pack.

My father's dream was to sell the store and open a small gallery with sculpture and paintings. My father could have been another Van Gogh. Or, at least, a portrait artist. He was really good with faces, especially eyes. He kept his easel in the store, right by the register, and when business was slow he sketched. There are charcoal drawings, most of them of our customers, hanging on a wire around the perimeter of the store. And upstairs, in my parents' bedroom, the walls are covered with portraits of us. Mom, Jason and me. A family history.

Hugh had been working in the store all summer. That's how we met. We didn't start going out right away, though. At first it was just me saying, "You want help stacking the bread?"

And Hugh answering, "Sure, why not?"

Hugh didn't say much. All I knew about him was that he was going to be a senior and that he liked his pizza with pepperoni. And I knew how I felt when I stood close to him. Or when he looked at me. Or when his hand brushed against my arm.

FIVE

One afternoon I am sitting in the living room, leafing through a magazine. I can't read anymore. I try, but the words blur together, or I find myself reading the same sentence over and over and still don't know what I have read. My mother and Jason are in their rooms, napping. We are getting to be experts at sleeping during the day. So when the doorbell rings, there is no one to answer it but me. And it is Hugh.

"How's it going, Davey?" he asks, as he hugs me.

Before I can answer, before I can lie and say, *okay,* Hugh begins to cry. I feel his body shaking and I back away, looking anyplace but at him.

I hear him sniffle and take a breath. "How about a walk on the beach?"

"No," I tell him.

"Your mother says you haven't been out of the house since the funeral."

"So?"

"So . . . it would be good for you to get outside."

My mother comes into the room then, pulling her robe around her. "That's what I've been trying to tell her," Mom says. "She needs some fresh air."

"Oh, all right," I say, seeing the pained look on Mom's face. I go into the bathroom and splash my face with cold water. I have dark circles under my eyes and my suntan has faded to a yellowish color. I pull my rope belt through my jeans, which are falling off because of all the weight I've lost since that night. I look like hell. But I don't care.

Outside, the bright sunshine hurts my eyes and I have to shade them with my hand. I follow Hugh down the stairs but I don't look at the store. I know there is a CLOSED sign on the door. I saw Walter printing it the day after the funeral.

Hugh takes my hand. He rubs his thumb along the bottom of mine, trying to soothe me. I know this is hard for him, too. I tighten my fingers around his, to let him know I understand. We walk to the Boardwalk, then across it, to the beach.

I take a deep breath and inhale the salt air which is mixed with the aroma of roasting peanuts, taffy and the musty smell of the amusement piers.

I was conceived on the beach, under the Million Dollar Pier. My parents used to call me their Million Dollar Baby. I'm the reason my father gave up his sports scholarship to Rutgers, and my mother went to work in a James' Saltwater Taffy shop. In those days Atlantic City was the pits. But not anymore. Now that gambling's been voted in, Atlantic City is supposed to become the next Las Vegas. Hotels and casinos are sprouting up all over the place.

"What are you thinking?" Hugh asks, as we walk along the ocean's edge.

"Nothing," I say.

And then Hugh puts his arms around me and kisses me. I want to kiss him back but I can't. I can't because kissing him reminds me of that night. So I break away from him and run. I hear Hugh calling, "Davey . . . wait."

But I don't wait. I run and run, until I am home. Then I get into bed and stay there for five days.

SIX

I don't want to start school. I don't want to do anything but stay in bed. Stay in bed, with the covers over my head. All day. At night I prowl around, carrying my breadknife, and I check the lock on the door and listen for footsteps. I try not to remember. Not to remember that night. Not to remember the brown paper bag on my closet shelf. Not to remember anything.

"Take a shower, Davey," my mother says, on the night before school starts. "Wash your hair. I'll bet it's been ten days. That's not like you."

It's been thirteen days. Thirteen days since I've bathed. I know I smell. But I don't care. I roll over and pull the bedsheet up over my ear. My bed smells too. I like it. A warm, salty, slightly sour smell. My own unwashed smell. Coming from the inside of me.

"Please, honey," Mom says. "Don't wait until tomorrow morning to get ready for school."

As if I am planning to jump out of bed in the morning and head right for the shower.

She shakes me a little to make sure I am listening. "For me, Davey. Do it for me, okay?"

It is the *for me* that gets through. My mother

doesn't pull guilt trips on me very often. And maybe she isn't even trying, but it works. There is still a side of me that feels badly for behaving the way I am. After all, I'm not the only one who cares about my father.

So I get out of bed, feeling wobbly from lack of exercise and so little food. And I head for the bathroom.

Minka follows me. She jumps onto the toilet seat and laps up water from the bowl. She has her own bowl of fresh water in the kitchen but there's something about drinking from the toilet that really appeals to her. I've given up on trying to get her to stop. Minka is a beautiful calico, with white paws. I got her for my twelfth birthday. She was the only female in the litter. Lenaya says Minka has an oral fixation. That she wasn't suckled enough as a kitten, so she's trying to make up for it now. It's true that she'll lick you. Fingers, toes, you name it. But that only makes her more lovable.

I wonder if Minka understands about my father. At times I think she does. That she senses something wrong. She's lost a lot of her playfulness since that night and spends most of her time curled in a ball, sleeping on my bed, next to my legs. Or maybe she is just trying to comfort me. Who knows?

I stand under the hot shower, soaping myself all over. I shampoo my hair twice and let the suds drip down into my face, stinging my eyes.

I used to sing in the shower. I like the way my voice sounds with an echo chamber. I wonder if I'll ever sing in the shower again? I wonder if I'll ever want to?

I wrap myself in a towel and walk down the hall to my room. My mother has changed the sheets on my bed.

"You didn't have to do that," I tell her.

"I know. I wanted to," she says. "You'll sleep better."

"I don't feel very well," I tell her. "I might be coming down with something." I get into bed and lie back on the clean pillowcase.

Mom sits down on the edge of my bed. "I remember my first day of high school," she says, tossing her hair away from her face. "I had violent stomach cramps. I didn't want to go either." She takes my hand in hers.

"It's not that," I say. "It's . . ."

"I know, Davey." Tears well up in her eyes. "Don't you think I know?"

"Yes," I tell her. "But having you know isn't enough."

The next morning, when I walk into the kitchen, Jason is wearing his Dracula cape and gobbling up his cereal. He can't wait to go back to school. "And this year I'm going to read real books. No more baby books. Right, Mom?"

"Right, Jase," Mom says, buttering her toast.

"And what else . . . what else will I learn?" Jason asks.

"Oh, a lot of interesting things," Mom says.

I stand in front of the open refrigerator, but nothing inside tempts me. Part of me is hungry, another part can't get the food down.

"What'd you learn in second grade, Davey?" Jason asks, his mouth full of Grape-nut Flakes.

"More of what I learned in first grade," I tell him. I close the refrigerator door. "You're not going to wear that cape to school, I hope."

"Why not? I like it."

"It makes you look like Dracula," I say.

"It's supposed to."

"Mom . . . do you think he should? I mean . . ."

"Oh, I think it's all right," Mom says. "If it makes Jason feel comfortable . . ."

"Comfortable," Jason repeats. He eats a piece of toast, then says, "What about the store, Mom? Are you going to open the store today?"

"Not today," Mom answers.

"When?" Jason asks.

"I don't know," Mom tells him.

My mother hasn't set foot in the store since that night. None of us has. I don't know what we're going to do.

I meet Lenaya at the bus stop and when the bus comes we find two seats together. It is crowded, with some kids standing in the aisle by the time we reach the next stop. I begin to get a closed-in feeling. It starts with my hands getting cold and clammy, then there is a queasiness in my stomach, and finally, I begin to feel dizzy, as if I might pass out. I put my head down to the floor.

"Are you okay?" Lenaya asks.

I can't answer.

She bends over, her mouth close to my ear. "Did you eat any breakfast?" she asks softly.

I shake my head.

"Here," she says, going through her lunch bag. "Eat this." She hands me an orange that has already been peeled.

I shove a piece into my mouth and bite into it, tasting the sweetness of its juice.

I feel better.

I make it through assembly, where the principal welcomes our class to the school, through a short homeroom session and through English, where Lenaya and I sit next to each other. She keeps looking at me, offering half smiles and once, she reaches over and touches my hand, which is trembling. But I hadn't known it until then.

After English, I am on my own, trying to find Room 314, where my geometry class is scheduled to meet. But I can't find it and I begin to feel frightened. I can hear each thump of my heart. I can't seem to catch my breath, so I breathe harder and faster, trying to get some air into my lungs, but it doesn't work. Nothing works. Groups of kids are coming toward me in the hall, laughing and talking. One of them could be the junkie who killed my father, I think. There is no evidence that the killer was a junkie, or even a kid, but that is what I believe.

I want to run. I want to run as far from school as I can. But I can't move. Can't get my feet going. Can't breathe. And then I pass out, hearing the thud of my head as it hits the floor.

Later, I am told that two girls and a boy helped me to the nurse's room.

The nurse assumes that I am having First-Day-in-High-School-Panic.

"It's not that," I try to explain from the cot where I am resting. I notice that my belt has been loosened and that my Adidas are arranged neatly under the cot.

"Then what?" the nurse asks. She is very pretty with dark hair, tied back, and gray eyes. She has an accent I can't place at first, but after a while I recognize it as Oklahoma, because my mother has a friend, Audrey, from Tulsa, and that's how she sounds.

"Growing up isn't easy," the nurse says, and I feel like laughing because she is so naïve. "A lot of us don't feel ready to leave the nest."

"No," I say. "You don't understand."

She smiles. "Oh, I think I do." She looks over my medical form, which our doctor had filled out the end of June, and reads, "No heart problems, no diabetes, no history of severe pain, or fainting spells, and normal periods. Well . . . no medical disorders at all." She smiles at me again and closes the folder. She walks across the room, puts the folder back in a filing cabinet and returns with a cup of water and two white pills. She hands them to me and says, "Down the hatch."

"What are they?" I ask, suspiciously.

"Aspirin."

"I don't have a headache."

"With that bump on your noggin?"

"It doesn't hurt," I say. "Unless I touch it."

"Even so . . ." she says, "let's go."

She is going to stand over me until I swallow the aspirin. I can tell. I might as well get it over with. So I sit up and take the pills.

"That's a good girl," she says, pulling a chair up to my cot. She sits down, adjusts her uniform over her knees, leans close and says, "Is it that time of the month, Davey?"

"No."

She looks at me for a while. I wish she would go away. Doesn't she have anything better to do on the first day of school? I wonder. Then she says, "Do you do drugs?"

I don't answer. I am offended by her question.

"Strictly off the record," she says. "Just between the two of us."

"No," I tell her. "I don't do drugs."

"You didn't get stoned last night?"

"No, I didn't."
"Booze?"
"No."
"Is there a chance you might be pregnant?"
"No."
"Not even a teensy-weensy chance?"
"Not even that," I say.

A boy comes into the room then and calls, "Nurse . . . I've got this incredible earache."

The nurse pulls the white curtains around my cot, giving me privacy. I hear her telling the boy that two aspirin will probably help. I close my eyes and drift off to sleep.

On the second day of school I pass out on my way to lunch. I am with Lenaya and she gets me to the nurse's room.

"Again?" the nurse says, clucking her tongue at me. "What are we going to do with you?"

When it happens on the third day of school, the nurse says, "You know what, Davey? I think it's time for you to see a doctor."

So Mom takes me to Dr. Foster's office. He listens to me as I explain what's been happening, gives me a quick examination, and tells me to get dressed and come into his office.

My mother and Dr. Foster are waiting for me there. On the doctor's desk is a picture of his wife and two sons, when they were small. They're older than I am now. He writes something on my chart, then he looks up and says,

"You're hyperventilating, Davey. Do you understand what that means?"

"I thought I've been fainting."

"It's different than fainting," Dr. Foster explains. "This is caused by the way you're breathing."

"I breathe that way because I feel like I *can't* breathe. I feel like I can't get any air at all."

"Yes, well . . ." Dr. Foster says, "we can all make ourselves hyperventilate. Divers do it . . . sprinters, before a race. You get a rush of oxygen to the brain. It can make you feel lightheaded."

"Why am I doing that?"

"Anxiety. You've been through a lot." He looks over at my mother, who is fastening and unfastening the clasp on her purse. Each time she does, it makes a clicking sound. Other than that the room is very quiet. "A new school . . . a tragedy in the family," Dr. Foster continues. "It's a lot to contend with at once."

I think it is interesting that he puts the new school before the tragedy.

"Of course, facing up to it is the best way of dealing with it." He rubs his eye. "Tell you what," he says, "let's give it another week. If you feel that you're beginning to hyperventilate, talk to yourself. Tell yourself that you're feeling anxious. That you have a right to feel anxious. Tell yourself to relax. Try to breathe slowly, regularly." He scribbles something on his prescription pad, rips it off, and hands it to me. "And I want you to take this high-potency vitamin, with minerals." He stands up. "A change of scene might do her good," he says to Mom. "It might do all of you some good . . . if it's possible."

"Thank you, Dr. Foster," Mom says. She always thanks him when we are leaving, as if he's doing us a favor by being our doctor.

"Anytime, Gwen," he says. "And I mean that."

"Yes, I know," Mom says.

He pats me on the shoulder. "You'll be all right, Davey. It takes time . . . that's all."

That night Mom phones Bitsy and Walter in New Mexico. "I'd like to take you up on your offer," she says. "Davey's been having some . . ." She pauses, trying to find the right word. "Some trouble," she says. "And the doctor has recommended a change of scenery."

When Mom gets off the phone she tells us that Bitsy and Walter are very glad that we're coming to visit.

"Do they have an ocean?" Jason asks.

"No, but they have mountains."

"How high?"

"Very high," Mom tells him.

"Can you fall off?"

"No."

"You're sure?"

"Yes."

Walter and Bitsy make all the arrangements

for our flight from Philadelphia to Albuquerque. They even arrange to have Minka travel in the cabin with me, instead of underneath, in the baggage compartment.

I worry about paying for the tickets because I know we don't have any extra money. Then Mom tells me that they have been pre-paid, by Walter and Bitsy. "Of course I'm going to pay them back," Mom says. "As soon as I get things organized."

We are going to leave in three days. I don't go back to school. It doesn't make any sense, when we'll be gone for more than two weeks. And Mom doesn't give me an argument about it so I guess that she agrees with me. I don't hyperventilate once in those three days. Instead, I think about the trip. About getting away. I try to picture New Mexico. I try to keep my mind from wandering back to that night.

Every morning Mom reminds me to take my vitamin. It is huge and hard to swallow. It also turns my pee green.

When we are on the plane, somewhere between Chicago and Albuquerque, I flush the rest of the vitamins down the toilet.

SEVEN

Bitsy and Walter meet us at the airport. The sky in Albuquerque is bright blue. Bright blue and perfect, without a cloud. I've never seen such a sky. I can't stop looking at it. I can't believe it is real. The sun is shining and it is hot, but not an Atlantic City kind of hot. Not sticky.

We climb into Walter's Blazer. Mom sits in front with Bitsy and Walter. Jason and I sit in the back. He is wearing his Dracula cape. He never takes it off. I think he even sleeps in it. I hold Minka on my lap. Behind our seat is an open area, where Walter has piled our luggage. When I turn around to make sure that neither my bag nor my knapsack has been left behind, I notice the rifle, or something that looks like a rifle. It is long and sleek. My heart begins to pound. "Uncle Walter," I say, "is that a gun in the back?"

"Yes," he answers.

"Is it loaded?" I ask.

"You bet . . . so don't go messing with it."

"Is there a lot of crime here?" I feel myself breathing harder, faster.

"No," Bitsy says. "And on The Hill . . ."

"The Hill?" I ask, interrupting.

"Yes," Bitsy says, "we call Los Alamos, The Hill . . . and up there we have virtually no crime at all."

"Then why do you carry a loaded gun?" I ask, telling myself to relax. Relax and try to breathe slowly, normally.

"You never can tell," Walter says, "especially down here. It's better to be safe than sorry."

I don't understand but decide not to pursue it because the whole subject is making me jumpy and every time I ask Walter a question, he turns and speaks to me over his shoulder, taking his eyes off the road.

I see my mother grab the back of her seat with one hand and hang onto the handle of her door, with the other.

"Walter!" Bitsy shrieks, as he swerves and just misses colliding with a passing car.

Jason crashes into me, laughing. "Daddy had a gun in the store. Right, Mom?"

"Right," Mom says, easing her grip on the back of the seat.

"But he didn't keep it loaded because he was afraid I'd want to play with it. Right, Mom?"

"Right, Jase. Now why don't you look out the window at the beautiful scenery."

"I *am* looking," he says. "I can talk and look at the same time."

The scenery *is* beautiful. We whisk by flat open spaces with mountains in the distance, rising out of nowhere, stark and black, looking as if they're made of papier-mâché. The land is brown, then yellow, then almost red.

After an hour on the road, Jason says, "I have to pee."

There are no gas stations, no restaurants, nothing, as far as you can see, except the land and the sky.

Walter pulls off the road and takes Jason for a short walk. When they come back, and we are on our way again, Jason falls asleep, with his head on my lap. He wakes up suddenly, not knowing where he is and I can read the fear in his eyes.

"It's all right," I tell him, smoothing his hair away from his sweaty cheek, where it has stuck.

I close my eyes, too, and when I awaken, I can feel the pull of the Blazer as we climb higher and higher. I have to yawn to clear my ears. "How much longer?" I ask Walter.

"Another fifteen minutes or so," Walter says, turning around to face me. I must remember not to talk to him while he is driving.

Minka jumps from one side of the Blazer to the other, chasing a little moth that has flown in the back window. I look at my watch: five-thirty. But I remember that that is New Jersey time. Here it is just three-thirty. I reset my watch.

We go around a series of S-curves, with a sheer drop of hundreds of feet to our right. Jason grabs my arm and squeezes so hard he leaves finger marks. Around and around, and I understand why Bitsy calls Los Alamos, The Hill.

Halfway up, Walter pulls off at a scenic lookout and we get out of the Blazer to stretch our legs and take in the view. All there is, for miles and miles, is a sea of rocky cliffs, dropping away into deep canyons. I don't know how I will ever describe this view to Lenaya and Hugh.

"You can understand why Oppenheimer chose Los Alamos as the site for Project Y," Bitsy tells Mom.

"What's Project Y?" Jason asks.

"The code name for building the atom bomb," Bitsy says. "And Los Alamos is the secret place where the scientists lived while they were developing it."

"Is it still a secret place?" Jason asks.

Bitsy laughs. "Not anymore."

Jason is disappointed.

We get back into the Blazer and drive a few more miles, until we come to the town itself. After the two hour drive, after the spectacular scenery, after hearing about the town as a secret place, I am disappointed, too. Los Alamos looks ordinary. Flat and ordinary. I once went to visit a friend's brother at Fort Dix, an army base in New Jersey, and Los Alamos reminds me of it. We could be anywhere, I think, as we drive past a shopping center, past the small library, past the post office. Anywhere at all.

We turn right, onto Diamond Drive, and Bitsy

points out the high school, a sprawling brown cinder block building. There are a lot of kids hanging out in the parking lot. They are dressed in T-shirts and jeans. I've forgotten that it is Thursday and that most kids are in school. I wonder what's going on at my school, in Atlantic City.

Then we turn left, and left again, and we pull into a driveway on a street where most of the houses look the same, with small, neatly mowed front lawns and rows of marigolds. Everything looks familiar to me, as if I have seen it all before, except for the mountains.

"Here we are!" Bitsy sings.

There is another car parked in front of the garage with a bumper sticker that reads, *I Love My Volvo.* Bitsy pats it on the way to the house and says, "This is *my* baby."

Walter carries in our bags, then goes back outside to hose down the Blazer, while Bitsy takes us on a tour of the house. She explains that it had been a government-built duplex but that she and Walter have renovated it, making it into a one-family house.

Inside, there is a huge living-dining room. The furniture is Early American and seems small, but only because the room is so big. There is a fireplace flanked by two sofas which are piled high with needlepoint pillows.

In the kitchen Bitsy opens the freezer and says, "We buy a side of beef every year."

Jason and I peer into the freezer. I expect to see half a cow, but instead there are just stacks of neatly wrapped packages, labeled *one pound ground meat, three pounds chuck roast.* There are also stacks of frozen vegetables, enough to last six months.

Upstairs, there are two wings. Bitsy shows us to ours, which consists of three small bedrooms and a bathroom. It's not very different from our house in Atlantic City. Bitsy and Walter have a bedroom and bath in the other wing.

"Supper on the deck in an hour," Bitsy says.

I close the door to my room and flop onto the bed with Minka. But Minka is anxious to explore and doesn't want to be held. She likes the little balls on the white chenille bedspread. On one wall there is a group of old photos. I study them for a long time before I realize they are of my father's family. Sometimes I forget that Bitsy is my father's sister. That they had the same parents.

There is a refinished trunk at the foot of my bed, with a yellow and white afghan folded over it. I toss the afghan onto the bed and open the trunk. It is empty. But it has been carefully lined with a paisley print material. If it were my trunk I'd keep special things in it, like my angora sweater set and my diary and my favorite books.

I decide to unpack, sure that I will feel better once I put my things away. I arrange my clothes in the dresser drawers and hang my dress and two jackets in the closet. I put the brown paper bag on the top closet shelf, over in the corner. I shove the breadknife under my pillow. There. Finished. I scoop up Minka and carry her downstairs.

The rest of the family is already outside. Jason is on the back lawn, tossing a Frisbee into the air; my mother is stretched out on a lounge chair on the deck, sipping a drink; Walter is dressed in a chef's apron and is cooking hamburgers on the grill; and Bitsy is flitting in and out of the house, carrying dinner plates, a wooden salad bowl, and a basket of fruit.

Suddenly I feel hungry. I don't know if it is the hour, the smell of charcoal broiled hamburgers, or what. But I haven't felt so hungry since before that night. I used to have this really intense appetite and Mom was always teasing me that I'd better watch it or I'd wind up fat. Not likely. I only weigh 101 and I'm 5′ 5″, and now, with all the weight I've lost I probably don't weigh more than 95.

Walter checks the meat and calls, "Jason . . . supper's on . . ."

Jason comes racing back to the deck and we sit down at the redwood table.

"Well," Bitsy says, waving her fork, "what do you think of our place?"

"It's beautiful," Mom says. But she sounds dreamy, as if she is talking about something else.

Bitsy sighs. "You know, Davey, when we

bought this house we expected to raise a family here, but . . . c'est la vie."

I don't respond. I don't know what to say.

"We tried for years," Bitsy continues. "We went through every test imaginable. Didn't we, Walter?"

"We did," Walter says.

"Of course, today they have so many new methods . . . but it's too late for us."

I think about my parents taking a chance just one time and wham . . . getting me. I wonder how Walter and Bitsy feel about that. I'm sure they know. And I wonder why they never adopted a baby if they wanted one so badly. But I don't ask. I finish my hamburger and reach for a second helping of potato salad.

"You see that apricot tree," Bitsy says, pointing. "We planted it the year we moved in. Isn't it beautiful?"

"Yes," we all answer at once.

"We're just so happy that you're here," Bitsy says, giving Mom's arm a pat. "And we want you to have a wonderful time."

Bitsy is talking as if we are really on vacation. As if everything is fine and dandy. As if we are just an ordinary family visiting their relatives and having supper on the deck.

No one mentions the real reason for our being here.

No one mentions my father.

For dessert Bitsy carries out a strawberry ice cream pie with a graham cracker crust.

"Yum," Jason says, tasting it, and licking his lips. "This is really good." He wolfs it down, then runs back into the yard, to play with his Frisbee.

Bitsy serves coffee to the rest of us. I never drink coffee but I accept a cup anyway, then disguise it with four sugars and pour cream up to the brim.

I half listen as Walter and Bitsy chat on about the town, their friends, all the interesting sights we are going to see.

And then, suddenly, Jason is crying, "Mommy . . . Mommy . . ." and running back to the deck, his hands over his face.

When he takes them away I see the blood. Blood, gushing—gushing and dripping onto his clothes, onto the deck. I panic and scream. I scream and I scream until Mom grabs me and shakes me by the shoulders and shouts, "Stop it, Davey! Stop it! It's just a nosebleed. That's all. A nosebleed." She hugs me tightly and my screams turn to sobs. "It's all right, honey," Mom says over and over again. "It's all right."

Bitsy shoves a glass under my nose and says, "Here . . . take a sip . . ."

I try to say, *What is it?* but I can't get the words out.

Still, Bitsy must understand because she says, "It's brandy. It'll make you feel better."

I take a sip and it burns my throat. Burns my

throat and makes me cough. I take a second sip anyway, then a third. It makes my stomach feel warm. I sit down and try to breathe normally.

"You sure can scream," Jason says. He is sitting on Walter's lap, an ice pack pressed to the back of his neck.

"It's the high altitude," Walter tells me. "Some people get nosebleeds when they first come here. He'll be fine."

"I'll be fine," Jason repeats. "Did you think I was going to die?"

"No, of course not," I answer.

"Then why did you scream that way?"

I shake my head, unable to answer.

EIGHT

A week later we are sitting around the dinner table when I ask Bitsy if I can borrow her bicycle tomorrow. I've seen two of them in the garage, each labeled *Kronick*, with their address, phone and social security numbers engraved across the bar.

"Certainly," Bitsy says, "as long as you wear a helmet."

"A helmet?" I ask.

"Yes. You can borrow mine." She finishes her third cup of coffee and wipes her mouth with a napkin.

"But I ride all the time in Atlantic City," I tell her, "and I never wear a helmet."

"That's the rule," Bitsy says as she stands up and stacks our plates.

"Really?" I say. "You're serious?" Of course I know that she is serious. But I have this idea that by questioning her I can make her change her mind.

"You bet I'm serious," she says.

So much for my idea.

"Okay. I'll wear the helmet." I will do anything to have some time to myself. Some time alone, to think.

"We'll be leaving for Cochiti Lake at ten-thirty. Just be sure you're back by then."

Cochiti Lake is number one on tomorrow's agenda. Walter has taken the week off so that he can show us the sights. So far we have visited Camel Rock, Bandelier National Monument, three Indian pueblos, Taos and the D. H. Lawrence Ranch.

But I don't think I can make it through another day of sightseeing with the family. This is a touchy subject, and I have to approach it carefully. So I clear my throat and say, "The truth is, I'd really like to beg off tomorrow. That is, if you don't mind." I look around the table for reactions. I can't tell what anyone is thinking so I continue. "I'd just like to ride around on your bicycle and maybe sunbathe on the deck . . ."

It is important that I don't insult them. They've been nice. But I'm sick of listening to Walter's lectures on everything from Black Mesa to black pottery, from solar energy to nuclear energy. He talks as if he is an expert on every subject. And who knows? Maybe he is.

Bitsy speaks first. "Well," she says, carefully, "rest and relaxation is what we were planning for next week, when Walter goes back to the Lab."

"But that's really what I need now," I say firmly, surprising myself.

"What do you think, Walter?" Bitsy asks.

Walter mulls it over as if world security is at stake. "Hmmm . . ." he begins. I fidget with the buttons on my shirt and wait. "I think it will be all right," he finally says, "if Davey promises to be very careful."

"Oh yes," I tell them. "I'll be very careful."

"Gwen . . ." Bitsy says, looking down the table, at Mom. "Is it all right with you?"

"What? Oh, yes . . . fine," my mother says. I get the feeling she doesn't even know what we are talking about. She seems distracted.

"And if Davey doesn't come with us I get the whole back seat of the Blazer to myself, right?" Jason says.

"Wrong!" Bitsy tells him. "I'm going to sit in the back and tickle you all the way to Cochiti."

"No!" Jason shrieks.

They have this game where Bitsy threatens to tickle Jason, but she never does. Jason is wildly ticklish. He becomes hysterical if you just wiggle your fingers close to his body, hinting that he might be in for it. I once read an article that said tickling is a form of torture. I wonder if Bitsy knows that.

NINE

The next morning I grab a piece of toast, go directly to the garage and walk Bitsy's bicycle out into the driveway in time to see Walter shoving his gun into the back of the Blazer. I am used to this by now. The gun automatically goes into the Blazer whenever Walter leaves The Hill. And as soon as he returns, the gun is removed. I don't know where he keeps it in the house. And I don't want to know.

"Bye, Uncle Walter," I call.

"Remember . . . ride with the traffic," Walter tells me. "That's a rule we observe on The Hill."

"With the traffic," I repeat.

"See you later, Davey."

"You bet," I call as I pedal away. *You bet* is Walt and Bitsy's favorite expression. Sometimes it means *yes,* sometimes it means *you're welcome.* Other times it seems to be a substitute for *okay*. This is the first time I have tried it.

As soon as I am out on Diamond Drive I stop and take off the helmet, shoving it into the canvas bike bag. I shake out my hair. There, that's better. What they don't know won't hurt them. I ride up Diamond Drive, past the high school. Groups of kids are hanging out in the parking lot. I have forgotten that it is Friday, another school day. Which reminds me of how many classes I'm missing. Sixteen days. Still, sixteen days at the beginning of the term isn't that bad. I bet I can catch up in a week, if I want to.

I pedal harder and faster, until my legs hurt. The pain begins in the backs of my calves and spreads up, into my thighs. My shoulders ache. But I don't care. I've been numb for so long the pain makes me feel alive again. I wish I could skip the whole school year. I bet I could keep up at home. I wish I *never* had to go back to school. What good does it do you in the long run?

I have trouble breathing, but not from hyperventilating. From the exercise. From the altitude. Everything is that much harder at 7,300 feet. Even breathing.

Sweat trickles down my face, stinging my eyes. It trickles down inside my T-shirt and along the backs of my knees, but I keep pedaling, past the Conoco Station, past the golf course, up the hill, until I come to an area of tall pine trees. I pull off the road and lean the bicycle against a tree. I make my way through the woods until I come to a beautiful canyon. I am still amazed at the scenery here. I half expect to hear hoofbeats in the distance, and then, to see a cowboy thundering into view, riding a slick, black stallion.

I sit on a rock, at the very edge of the canyon, hugging my knees and looking down. The rock juts out and makes me feel I could fly right off it.

How quickly everything can change, I think. One minute you're alive and the next, you could be dead. There isn't any way to know what's going to happen. If this rock comes loose, I'll fall, I think. Fall to the bottom of the canyon. Will I fall straight down, I wonder, or kind of float down, gently? Either way my head will smash open and my bones will break. How long will it be before I am found? Days, weeks, a month? Maybe I'll never be found. Then the buzzards will pick at my flesh until there is nothing left of me. Nothing, but bones. Broken bones.

I shake that image from my mind and concentrate on the beauty of the canyon. I think about being at the bottom, surrounded by it. I am tempted to climb down but then I remember Bitsy's story about the fourteen-year-old boy who was killed by a falling rock while he was climbing in a canyon. And about the woman who tripped and fell, breaking her leg. By the time she was found she was in shock and didn't make it.

Bitsy and Walter are full of stories about what might happen. They don't believe in taking chances. They will probably live to be one hundred.

I decide to climb down anyway. I don't know whether to go backwards, hanging onto the rocks or to try walking down, frontwards. I combine the two methods and get going.

Down, down I climb, rock after rock, losing my footing every now and then, grabbing hold of a branch to steady myself.

Down, down, traveling over the steepest inclines on my backside.

Down, down.

I don't know how long it takes me. Half an hour? An hour? I've left my watch at home, knowing that today there is no schedule to follow. That today is mine.

Down, down, into the bottom of the canyon.

I look up now, surprised at how far I have come and for a second I remember that I will have to climb back up, that I shouldn't go too far. Then, I am distracted by a lizard. How perfectly he blends into his surroundings. I stand there and watch as he scampers from rock to rock. I stretch out on a rock myself, lifting my face to the sun, and a feeling comes over me. A feeling of wanting to share all of this with my father. I want to talk with him so badly I ache. I want to tell him how I climbed down into the canyon by myself. That I wasn't afraid. I want to tell him everything. Everything that has happened since that night. Everything I am thinking and feeling.

I wish I could feel his kiss on my forehead again, light and loving. I wish I could feel his hand smoothing my hair away from my face. His hands were so big. Big enough to palm a basketball. Big enough to hold Jason in the air.

I remember how warm it felt to be near him. How safe.

Suppose it's all been a mistake, I think. Suppose he's not dead at all. That when we get back to Atlantic City he'll be there, working in the store. And he'll say, *Well . . . well . . . if it isn't Davey Wexler . . .*

And I'll say, *In the flesh.*

And then we'll laugh. And I will never be too busy to go walking on the beach with him, or to help him in the store, or just to sit quietly at his side, again.

Oh Daddy, please don't be dead. Please!

And then it hits me. The realization that I'll never be with him again. Never. That he isn't coming back.

You have to face reality, Davey. You have to accept the facts.

I sit up and cup my hands around my mouth. "Daddy . . ." I call.

I hear my echo around the canyon. *Daddy . . . Daddy . . . Daddy . . .*

I stand up and call louder. "Can you hear me, Daddy? Can you?"

Then I hear a voice, answering mine and it isn't my echo.

"Hey . . . hey down there," it calls.

I spin around, trying to find it.

"Hey . . . are you all right?"

I catch a glimpse of him. He is standing halfway up the canyon and is partly hidden by a tree.

"Who . . . me?" I ask, as if it might be someone else.

"Yeah . . . you," he calls, as he begins to climb down. I shade my eyes from the sun and see that he is very sure footed. He is not slipping or sliding or falling, the way I did.

He reaches the bottom quickly and comes toward me. He is about nineteen or twenty, wearing faded cut-offs, hiking boots with wool socks sticking out over the tops and no shirt. He has a knapsack on his back. He is maybe 5′ 9″, with suntanned skin and dark hair.

"I thought you were in trouble," he says. "The way you were calling . . ."

His eyes are dark brown.

"No," I say. "I'm fine."

"What are you doing down here?" He sounds less friendly now.

"Thinking," I tell him. "Is there a law against that?" The truth is, I am scared out of my mind. My heart is pounding. Suppose he's a crazy, I think. Suppose he's a rapist or worse. If he is, I'm in for it. I have to prepare myself. There's no way I'm going to let him take me by surprise. I know what to do. I'll smash his head in with a rock. *A rock.* I have to find the right rock. I scan the ground and see a good one, not ten feet away. I move toward it, slowly, wishing I had my breadknife with me.

"No law against thinking," he says, "except that you're alone."

He's probably a junkie. He probably comes to the canyon to shoot up, I think, or to trip or just to get stoned.

"So . . . I'm alone," I say, sounding bitchier by the minute. "Is there a law against that?" I am standing right in front of the rock now. All I have to do is bend over, pick it up, and wham . . .

"No, but there should be," he says.

"Oh, yeah . . . why?" I am having trouble following our conversation but I know it is best to keep him talking. The longer he talks the less likely that he'll attack. I read that somewhere.

"Who's going to get help if you need it?" he asks me.

I think that's an interesting question, coming from him. I keep my eye on the rock. Every muscle in my body is tensed and ready to spring into action, if necessary.

"Suppose you trip and fall . . ." he begins.

"Suppose you do? You're alone too, aren't you?" Yes, that's good. Put some fear into him. Let him think that maybe *I'm* the crazy, waiting, waiting to pounce on him in the silence of the canyon.

"I've had plenty of experience," he says.

"And how do you know I haven't?"

Then he laughs. His teeth are very white

against his suntanned skin. "You don't know your ass from your armpit," he says.

Elbow, I think. He means elbow. "Listen, Machoman," I say, looking him in the eye. "Buzz off!" I sound really tough.

But all he does is laugh again. "Are you always so bitchy?"

"No," I say. "Just when I feel like it."

"You're new around here." He says this as a statement, not a question.

"So what if I am?"

"Hey, relax . . . I'm not going to bite you. All I'm trying to say is next time, bring a friend. It's safer that way."

"I don't have any friends."

"Find some," he tells me. He bends over and I panic, thinking that he is going for my rock. That he is going to use it on me. But all he does is pick up a handful of stones. He jiggles them around in his hand. Then, without looking at me he says, "Who are you so pissed off at, anyway?"

"The world!" I tell him, without even thinking about it. I am surprised by my answer to his question and by the anger in my voice. It is the first time I realize I am not only sad about my father, but angry, too. Angry that he had to die. And angry at whoever killed him.

He sits down on a rock, opens his knapsack and pulls out a bottle of water. I watch, as he takes a swig. I am so thirsty I can hardly stand it. The inside of my mouth is dried out. My tongue feels thick and furry. I would do anything for a drink of water.

He must sense this because he looks at me and says, "You're thirsty."

"A little," I tell him, licking my parched lips.

"You came into the canyon without a water bottle."

"I forgot it," I lie. "It's home."

"Here . . ." He passes his to me. I am so relieved I feel like crying. I mean to take a quick swig, but once it's to my lips I can't stop. I drink and drink until he takes it from me.

"Easy," he says, "or you'll get sick."

I begin to relax. He's not out to get me after all.

"What's your name?" I ask him.

"You can call me Wolf."

"Is that a first name or a last name?"

"Either," he says.

"Oh." I can't think of anything else to say.

He stands, puts the water bottle back into his knapsack, stretches and says, "Okay . . . let's go."

"Go?" I shouldn't have let down my guard. "Where?"

"Back up," he says. "It's one o'clock. I've got an appointment at two."

"So, go," I tell him.

"You're going with me."

"Really!" I say.

"Yeah . . . really."

"Guess again," I say.

"I'm not about to leave you down here by yourself. I'm not in the mood to be called by Search and Rescue later. I have other things to do."

"Search and Rescue?"

"Right."

I think about the fourteen-year-old boy who was killed by a falling rock and about the woman who broke her leg and went into shock and I wonder if Wolf was called in then. But I don't ask him. Instead I say, "I'm tougher than I look."

"Sure you are. Let's go. I'm in a hurry."

"How do I know I can trust you?"

"You see anybody you can trust more?"

I look around. He begins to walk away. I decide to follow him.

He climbs quickly. I try to step exactly where he does.

After a while I ask him if he goes to school around here.

He doesn't answer.

I say it again, louder. "You go to school around here, Wolf?"

"The more you talk the harder time you're going to have climbing," he says, without turning around.

Okay, I think. So I'm having trouble keeping up. So I'm breathing hard. So I'm a little out of shape. So what? I don't say any of this. Instead I watch the muscles in his legs. I notice how brown and smooth the skin is on his back, how his hair hangs just past the nape of his neck, how narrow his hips are, how strong his arms and shoulders look.

As if he knows what I am thinking, he turns. "How're you doing?"

"Okay. Just fine. I told you, I'm tough." I wipe the sweat off my face with the back of my hand.

Wolf turns and begins to climb again.

I follow him, then trip on a rock and skin my knee. I feel like crying out but I don't. I have to hurry to catch up with him. He doesn't seem to notice.

Finally, we reach the top and Wolf walks me to my bicycle and then, out to the road. I wonder if I will have the strength to ride home, then I remember that it will be almost all downhill.

Wolf leans against a tree, chewing on a piece of grass.

"Well, thanks," I say. "Thanks for the water and the guided tour."

He nods. We are both quiet for a minute. Then he says, "Get yourself a decent pair of boots. Adidas are okay for tennis, not rock climbing. And next time, bring a water bottle."

I get on my bicycle.

"What's your name?" he asks me, as I am about to pedal away.

I think for a minute before answering. When I do I face him and say, "You can call me Tiger."

"Is that a first name or a last name?" he asks.

"Neither!" I say and this time I do pedal away. I know that he's watching me, but I don't turn around. I can hear him laughing.

And I laugh too.

TEN

At home I gobble up the chicken sandwich Bitsy has left for me, then I take a hot shower. I am stiff and sore all over but I feel good. I begin to sing. I sing song after song, glad that no one is home to hear me, or see how much hot water I am using. I shampoo my hair, I scrub between each toe, and all the time I am singing. I think about quitting school and trying for a singing career. I can see it now—my name in lights on a revolving sign outside the Resorts International Hotel and Casino. Inside, the MC announces my debut: *Ladies and gentlemen . . . presenting Atlantic City's own Davey Wexler!* The drums roll. I step out on stage wearing this long, slinky black dress, slit up one side, my hair flowing down my back, a rose tucked behind my ear. I pick up the microphone and the room gets so quiet you can hear the snap of my fingers as I begin to sing in this husky, sexy voice that is nothing like the soprano I am in chorus. My mother sits out front at the best table with Jason, Lenaya and Hugh, sipping champagne.

Across the room, at a table by himself, is Wolf. I can't take my eyes off him. It seems I am singing every song just for him. When I finish, the audience goes wild, yelling *encore, encore.* I sing two more songs. After, Wolf rushes up to the stage and presents me with a bouquet of roses. Dozens of them. Pure white.

My mother and Jason, Lenaya and Hugh are all wondering who this stranger is. This stranger who is obviously so crazy about Davey.

ELEVEN

While I am drying off I begin to think about the shower I'd taken on the night my father was killed . . . I was sandy from the beach. And it was so hot and sticky that even the cool shower didn't help much.

The window air conditioner in the living room was on full blast and in both back bedrooms, fans were whirring. We had just one small lamp on, though, trying to conserve some energy, because the whole east coast had been warned of a possible brown-out.

Jason was racing around in his bathing suit and Dracula cape, fighting an imaginary war with his model airplanes. "Wham . . . got you. Pow pow pow . . . got you back . . ."

"Hurry up, Jase," my mother called. "Get into some clothes or we'll miss the sale." She was taking Jason to the Jean Machine. They were running a pre-season special on back-to-school clothes.

"Davey, would you zip me up?" Mom asked, knocking on my bedroom door.

I flipped over my Bruce Springsteen tape and danced across the room to the door. Mom, tall, slim and barefooted, backed into my room. I zipped her white sundress and fastened the little hook on top. She was carrying her sandals and her wet hair hung loose around her shoulders. She smelled of Ivory soap and baby powder. My hair was dripping down my back and I still had only a bath towel wrapped around me while I tried to decide what to put on to go walking with Hugh.

"Your nose is peeling again," Mom said.

I touched it. "I know."

"Keep it covered with zinc for a couple of days. Give it a chance to clear up."

"Zinc's disgusting. I'd rather peel."

"We should be back by ten," Mom said, forgetting about my nose, "unless we stop for ice cream . . . but by eleven at the latest."

"Okay."

She checked her watch. It was pink gold with a tiny ruby on each side of the face, a raised crystal and a narrow gold linked band. It belonged to my grandmother, who died fifteen years ago, right before I was born. Mom has had plenty of experience in dealing with death. Her father died when she was still in high school and her brother died when he was nineteen. So she named me Davis because there was no one else to carry on her family name.

"Jason, will you *please* put something on," Mom said again. She turned back to me. "Don't stay out too late. I'd rather have you bring Hugh back here . . . it's a lot safer than the beach."

As soon as Mom and Jason left I closed the door to my bedroom and as I got dressed I chatted with Minka.

"What we have here, Minka," I said, pulling on my favorite jeans, "is pure physical attraction. Physical Attrac-ti-on. You know what that means? It means it feels good to be near Hugh. *Really* good. When he holds my hand my insides flip over. Did you ever feel that way, Minka? Did some boy cat ever rub up against you and make you feel wonderful?"

Minka, who had been bathing, looked up. I scratched her under her chin, then put on my new halter.

"Well, don't you worry," I said. "It's never too late."

Minka gave me a big yawn.

I sprayed myself with *Charlie,* checked myself in the mirror, and ran downstairs, to the store, to wait for Hugh.

My father was at his easel, working on a portrait. There were no customers. He had the radio turned in to WFLN, the classical music station.

"Hi . . ." I said, helping myself to a peppermint candy from the glass bowl on the check-out counter. The sign on the bowl read, *Help the Retarded. Two for a Quarter.*

My father opened the cash register, took out a

quarter and dropped it into the bank behind the box.

Then he looked at me. "Well, well, well . . . if it isn't Davey Wexler . . ."

"In the flesh," I said.

"So I see," Dad said, eyeing my skimpy halter.

I felt my cheeks turn red.

I walked behind the counter to where Dad was sitting at his easel and looked over his shoulder. "Very nice . . ." I said. "Especially the eyes. I wish I could draw like you."

"You can do other things."

"Oh yeah . . . like what?"

My father pretended to think that over. "You're very good at stacking the bread," he said.

"Thanks a lot!"

We both laughed. I hung my arms over his shoulders, from behind, and rested my face against his hair, which was soft and curly and smelled of salt water.

"So, where are you off to?" Dad asked.

"Oh . . . Hugh and I are going out."

"What time will you be back?"

"I'm not sure."

"An educated guess."

"Ten . . . eleven . . . something like that."

"Stay off the beach. It's not safe at night."

"I've already had the lecture."

"I just don't want you to get carried away and forget."

"I won't. I promise."

"Well, I can't ask for more than that."

Hugh came into the store then, wearing his *Grateful Dead* T-shirt and jeans. "Hi everybody," he said. "Have you heard the one about the man who gave his cat a bath . . ."

"Stop," Dad said. "I've heard it two dozen times, from you."

Hugh walked up to the counter and took two mints, dropping a quarter into the bank.

"Ready?" he asked me.

"Ready. Bye, Dad. See you later."

"Bye," Dad said. "Have a nice time. And don't be too late."

"Don't worry, Mr. Wexler," Hugh said.

Outside the sun was setting.

TWELVE

Stop! I tell myself. Stop thinking about that night. Concentrate on how good it feels to be alive. No matter what. Just to see the color of the sky, to smell the pine trees, to meet a stranger in the canyon.

I go to my room, tear a piece of paper from the yellow pad on my dresser and write one word. *Alive.* Then I tear off another piece and write *Wolf.*

I get pleasure from seeing my hand form the letters. I write it in all caps. *WOLF.* I write it in all lower case letters. *wolf.* I spell it backwards. *flow.* I'm surprised to find that it spells a word. *Davey and Wolf. Wolf and Davey.* I open the trunk at the foot of the bed and place both pieces of paper inside it, on the paisley lining. Then I decide to put my angora sweater set in there too, on top of the papers. And my fisherman's pullover. Also, the letter from Lenaya, which she wrote and mailed on the day we left Atlantic City. And then the breadknife. I've been hiding it under my bed every morning but if Bitsy decides to vacuum and moves the bed, she'll find it, and that will mean questions and more questions. Better to keep it in the trunk during the day and to take it out only at night, when I might need it.

At dinner Mom asks me how my day was.

"Very interesting," I tell her. I see Bitsy raise her eyebrows. "And relaxing," I add, hoping to avoid any questions. "How was Cochiti Lake?"

"Very nice," Mom says. "Walter explained the whole history of the area to us."

I'll bet he did, I think.

"It's a man-made lake," Jason says. "And it's big enough to sail a boat."

"A small boat," Walter says.

"A small boat," Jason repeats.

"You missed a nice day, Davey," Bitsy tells me.

I hide my smile in a glass of milk.

Later, I sit with Jason on the deck. We snuggle together in one lounge chair, star gazing. The sky is so clear here that without any trouble I can make out the Dipper. I am able to find Cassiopeia, too. Walter is so impressed with what he considers my interest in astronomy that he has given me a book: *The Beginners Guide to Stars and Planets.*

"Look, Jason," I say. "There's Cygnus. The swan. Can you make out the neck . . . the wings?"

"I think so," Jason says, yawning. "I *want* to."

Impulsively, I hug him.

"Watch it," he says.

THIRTEEN

Two nights before we are due to fly home the phone rings. Walter answers. It is Audrey, my mother's friend from Atlantic City. "She probably wants to pick us up at the airport," Mom says, taking the call in the kitchen.

But when she comes back to the living room her face is deadly pale. "The store has been attacked by vandals," she says, quietly. "They shot out the windows and the inside is a mess. They smashed everything they could get their hands on."

Who would do such a terrible thing to us? I think. What have we ever done to anybody?

"The police have no leads," Mom continues. "But they don't think it's related to the robbery . . . to the . . ." Her voice trails off. She manages to say, "To the last time," before she covers her face with her hands.

The room is filled with the sound of a long, low wail. It sends shivers down my back. I look around, trying to identify it, then realize it is coming from my mother.

"Damn them!" she screams. "Damn them to hell!"

I know how she feels. I want to comfort her. To hold her close the way she held me when Jason had his nosebleed. But she is hysterical now, raving and ranting around the room, pulling at her own hair, screaming and crying and flinging aside whatever is in her way. Needlepoint cushions fly into the air, a stack of books is swept off the table with one movement of her arm, an amber glass ashtray smashes against the fireplace.

Jason stands in front of the grandfather clock, his hands over his ears. I can tell he is afraid. I am frightened, too. But even more, I am surprised. I've never seen my mother lose control. Not the night my father was killed, not at his funeral, not ever.

Until now.

Mom knocks over a lamp. I wait for Walter or Bitsy to stop her. Why are they just standing there like zombies? Why doesn't somebody do something! But then Mom kicks the wall with her bare foot and cries out in pain. She has hurt herself. The shock is enough to stop her. She begins to cry, but now it is a different kind of crying. She collapses against Bitsy, who takes her in her arms.

"I'm sorry," Mom whimpers. "I'm sorry . . . but I just can't take any more. I just can't . . ."

"Mommy . . ." Jason runs to her. "Mommy . . . don't do that again."

"I won't," Mom says, holding him close. "I

just couldn't help myself this time." She looks over at me. I look back, trying to let her know I understand, without saying a word.

Three of Mom's toes turn blue and swollen. Bitsy gets an ice pack. Mom yelps when Walter tries to touch her foot. They discuss whether or not they should go to the emergency room for X rays. They decide against it.

"There's nothing to do for broken toes but tape them together," Bitsy says. She once took a first aid course and this is what she learned. Besides, Mom doesn't want to go. She's embarrassed.

But the next day the pain is worse and Bitsy takes Mom for X rays anyway. Two of the toes are broken. The doctor tapes them together. Bitsy is pleased that her treatment was correct. Mom hobbles around in a pair of old tennis shoes with a hole cut out for her toes.

She can't decide what to do about the store. She can't decide what to do about anything. Walter and Bitsy convince her to stay a while longer.

"I'll take care of everything," Walter promises.

The next morning I walk down to Central Avenue and buy two postcards in TG&Y. One shows an aerial view of Los Alamos. *Greetings from the Atomic City* is printed across it. This one I will send to Lenaya. The other is a photo of Camel Rock at sunset. This one is for Hugh.

I cross the street and go to the post office,

where I write messages on each of the cards. *Hi, Future Scientist,* I write to Lenaya. And then I can't think of anything else I want to say. So I write in big letters. *Lots to tell you. See you soon.*

I address the Camel Rock card to Hugh and write *Did you hear about the store? It's the last straw. I don't know when we're coming home now.*

I mail the cards, then remember that I haven't signed either one of them. Oh well. They'll know they are from me.

I decide to go to the library since it is next to the post office. I browse around, picking a book off the best seller shelves, skimming it, then putting it back. I don't see anything I want to read. Nothing interests me. I'm having trouble concentrating, except on my star book. I am able to memorize what I read in that.

Outside, I pass a shoe store and in the window is a pair of hiking boots. They are on sale for $32.50, marked down from $59.95. I go in and ask to try them on.

The saleswoman tells me they are a very good buy, and asks what size I wear.

"Eight," I tell her. "Eight, narrow."

She goes into the back room and comes out carrying a big box, which she sets down on the floor. She whips off the cover and holds one boot up. "Vibram soles," she says. "The real McCoy."

I nod, as if I understand.

When she sees that I am wearing my Adidas

barefooted she reaches over for a basket filled with socks. "Let's see," she says, rummaging through it. "We want to see how they fit with heavy socks . . . wool would be best . . ." She shakes out a heavy gray sock. "Put this on, dear, and we'll see how they fit."

It is the same kind of sock Wolf was wearing. I pull it onto my left foot because I know that that one is slightly bigger than my right. The saleswoman helps me into the boot. It is stiff. She laces it up and tells me to stand.

"How does that feel?" she asks.

"I can't tell," I say. "I think I should try on the other one, too."

She looks in the basket for a matching sock. There is none. Instead, she hands me a pink knitted sock. I pull it on, wondering whose sock it was. I think about a girl, my age, taking off her pink sock to try on a pair of summer shoes, then forgetting it. Maybe that's how it wound up in the stray sock basket.

I get up and walk around in both boots, feeling as if my feet are encased in cement.

"You have to break them in," the saleswoman says. "Wear them around the house, wear them to school, get them nice and comfortable before you wear them hiking."

I turn around in front of the mirror.

"A terrific buy," she tells me again. "And you can weatherproof the suede. It will turn the color darker, but I think they look even nicer that way."

The feet I am looking at in the mirror seem to belong to someone else. They don't look like my feet at all.

"And the sale ends this Saturday," she reminds me.

But she doesn't have to worry. I have already made up my mind. I made it up the minute I saw them in the window. "I'll take them," I tell her. "And I'd like a pair of wool socks."

"Certainly, dear. White or gray?"

"Gray."

"And a bottle of Sno-Seal so you can weatherproof them right away?" she asks, reaching up to a shelf lined with Sno-Seals.

"Yes."

"And will that be all?"

"Yes."

"Cash or charge?"

"Cash," I say, opening my wallet. I have exactly $74.68 saved up from my summer job. I worked as a beach girl at the Park Place Hotel, handing out towels and carrying chairs for guests. I was paid in tips. On a good day I could pocket $15. I had planned to blow it all on a back-to-school shopping spree. Once I was shopping in Bamberger's with my mother and I saw this girl piling up sweaters and skirts and jeans and shirts. I couldn't take my eyes off that pile. And I guess she noticed because she turned to me and smiled. "I'm going away to college," she said, as if she had to explain. And I just smiled back and thought about what it must be like to have so much money that you can buy whatever you want, more, much more than you need. And that's what I'd planned to do with my $74.68, although I knew I wouldn't get much of a pile.

I hand my money to the saleswoman, who never stops smiling. "Thank you, dear," she says. Normally I'm put off by anyone who calls people *dear* yet she sounds as if she really means it and looks as if she is glad I came in and bought the hiking boots. She isn't just putting it on. Maybe it's because I am the only customer. Maybe business is slow this fall. Who knows?

On the way home I am hit with the guilties. What will my mother say? *A waste. What are you going to do with hiking boots in Atlantic City, Davey? Did you think it over carefully or was it just impulse buying? You know how hard it is to make ends meet, and especially now, with Daddy . . .*

Never mind. I won't show them to my mother, or to anyone else. They will be my secret. All I can think of is going to the canyon, finding Wolf, and showing him my hiking boots. Actually, all I can think about is going to the canyon and finding Wolf. I want to see if being around him still makes me feel glad to be alive.

I want to go this afternoon, right after lunch, but Bitsy has other plans. We haven't been to the

Bradbury Science Mu[illegible]
teer guide there every [illegible]
is Wednesday we will [illegible]

Bitsy wears a red ja[illegible]
says *Elizabeth Kronick*[illegible]
pants and a white shi[illegible]
She explains that there[illegible]
guides at the museum[illegible]
wears every week. It makes her *feel* official.

I am not too hot on going to the science museum but Jason can't wait. We walk over. It is another beautiful afternoon. The air is clear, the sky is a perfect blue color, the sun warming, yet through it you can feel just a hint of fall. My mother limps a little but her toes aren't giving her that much trouble. She doesn't say much. I hope she's going to be okay. I hope she's not going to explode again.

Bitsy whisks us through the museum and out to a courtyard where there are replicas of the atom bomb. There is a sign saying: *Displayed here are ballistic cases like those of the two atomic bombs detonated over Japan in August 1945, the only atomic weapons ever used in warfare. Each was the equivalent of about 20,000 tons of TNT. The result of twenty seven months of unprecedented effort by thousands of scientists and technicians, they represent one of the greatest scientific achievements of all time. Both bombs were designed, fabricated, and assembled at Los Alamos.*

Jason is really turned on by the bombs. He runs his hand along the surface of the one called Little Boy, which was dropped on Hiroshima. "And they were invented here, in Los Alamos?"

"That's right," Bitsy tells him.

"And they killed a lot of people?"

"Yes."

"How many people did this bomb kill?"

"A lot," Bitsy says.

"Hundreds?" Jason asks.

"Yes."

"Thousands?"

"Yes, I don't know the exact numbers."

I think it's peculiar for a guide not to be able to answer Jason's question. Maybe it is that she doesn't *want* to answer him.

"Does Uncle Walter make bombs?" Jason asks.

"Uncle Walter doesn't make them," Bitsy says. "He's involved in designing . . . and research."

"He is?" I say. "For bombs?"

"For weapons in general," Bitsy says.

"I had no idea," I say.

"You know Uncle Walter is a group leader in W Division," Bitsy says, proudly.

"But I don't know what W Division is," I say.

"It's the weapons division," Bitsy tells me. "Half of the Lab is involved in weapons research and the other half is involved in basic research. Medicine, energy . . ."

Bitsy is ticking off a list but I have tuned her out. I am thinking of Walter, instead. I can't picture him designing bombs. I always thought a person who designs weapons would be hard and cruel. A kind of wild-eyed mad scientist, intent on blowing up the world. But Walter is so ordinary. I just can't get over the fact that he is somehow involved in building bombs. In killing people.

A tourist couple asks if they can take a picture of Jason standing next to the replica of the bomb called Fat Boy, the bomb we dropped on Nagasaki. Jason poses and smiles.

That night, while we are having dinner, my mother develops an intense headache. "It's been coming on all day," she tells us, excusing herself from the table.

Maybe that's why she was so quiet in the museum this afternoon. She didn't say three words.

"I think I'd better take some aspirin and go to bed," she says.

"You'll feel better in the morning," Bitsy calls after her. "It's probably just the altitude." The altitude is Bitsy's excuse for every problem.

But I am not thinking about my mother or her intense headache. I am still thinking about Walter. I look at him differently now. I feel myself tensing up, growing more hostile toward him by the minute.

As if he can read my mind he leans across the table and says, "Davey . . . what's wrong?"

"Nothing," I manage to say.

"Oh yes." He gives me a scrutinizing look. "I can tell . . . something is wrong."

"Well," I begin. "It's just that I can't believe you design weapons."

"Oh, so that's it."

"Yes. I'm surprised."

"It's my job," he says. "And I do it as well as I can."

"Couldn't you find another job?" I ask.

"That's not the point."

"What is?"

"We're in this business to design the best weapons we can, so that no one will ever think they can win a war against us."

"That doesn't make any sense."

"Think of us as watchdogs, Davey, making sure that no one will ever attack us. But if they do, we'll be ready. And being ready is more than half the battle."

"But if nobody made bombs in the first place . . ."

"I wish it could be that way."

"Why can't it?"

"Because that's not the way of the world."

"It should be."

"You're right," Walter says. "But it's not."

Later, when I am in bed, I try to think of Walter as a watchdog, but the only picture I get in my mind is of a German shepherd, or a Doberman, named Walter. I imagine Walter sitting at his desk at the Lab, thinking up new ways to kill people. Walter, who hoses down the Blazer every time he drives it off The Hill. Walter, who helps clear away the dinner plates. Walter, who reads Jason a chapter from *Stuart Little* every night.

I tuck the breadknife under my pillow and sleep with one hand wrapped around it.

FOURTEEN

The next day I sneak my hiking boots down to the garage and bury one in each of Bitsy's canvas bike bags. I find a canteen on a shelf, rinse it and fill it with water.

When I go back to the house Jason is sitting on the living room floor playing Dominoes and Mom is stretched out on the sofa, twirling a rubber band around her fingers. Bitsy is in the kitchen. She tells me that she is going to a Bridge party and will be gone for lunch. "Do you want me to make you a sandwich before I leave?" she asks.

"No, don't worry about me. I'm going out for my exercise."

If I put it that way Bitsy doesn't object. She and Walter are very big on exercise. Walter jogs every day at noon and Bitsy leaves the house every morning at eight, for a brisk walk around the block with her friends. So there is no problem as long as I promise to wear the helmet and to ride facing traffic.

"Where do you go, Davey?" Bitsy asks, as she covers a freshly baked apple pie with aluminum foil.

"Oh, around," I say. "I like to explore."

"Just be careful. And don't take any chances."

"Me . . . take chances?" I picture myself climbing down into the canyon. "Don't worry. I don't take chances."

"Good," Bitsy says. "I'm glad to hear it. This family has had enough trouble."

"You bet," I say.

Bitsy gives me a strange look as I say goodbye to Mom and Jason. Maybe I haven't used her favorite expression in the right way.

When I reach the wooded area near the canyon, I lean my bike against a tree, sling the canteen over my shoulder, and exchange my Adidas for my boots, which are weatherproofed and ready for action. Then I traipse around in the woods, trying to get used to them. I walk in circles, alternately stomping, skipping, and jumping, then laughing, because I feel so silly. Finally, I head for the canyon.

I look down and hope I will see Wolf. But there is no one in sight. I sit for a while, thinking about Atlantic City and the beach. I used to go walking on the beach every day, winter and summer. It was my time alone, my time for thinking. Often I'd sit on a jetty and before I knew it an hour or more had passed. This canyon reminds me of the jetty, and the beach. It is a good place to be alone. A good place for my thoughts.

I see someone moving below me. I stand up

to get a better look. It is Wolf, making his way down into the canyon. "Hey . . ." I call. "Hey, down there . . ."

He turns but he can't see me. His eyes are blinded by the sun.

"You must be new around here," I shout. "I'll bet you don't know your ass from your armpit."

He moves away so that he is out of the sun's direct rays. He looks up and around. Still, he hasn't seen me.

"Suppose you get hurt," I say. "Who's going to call the Search and Rescue team?" I wave my arms like crazy until I am sure he has spotted me.

He laughs then and his laugh echoes through the canyon.

I scamper down to where he is standing, losing my balance just once.

Wolf looks me over and nods. "I see you found your canteen," he says.

"Uh huh."

"And got yourself a pair of hiking boots."

"Uh huh."

"Very good."

He leads the way and together we climb down into the canyon.

By the time we get there my right boot is making a blister across the heel of my foot. I should have brought some Band-Aids with me.

At the bottom we sit on a rock and watch the lizards racing around. Minka would be very happy down here, I think. She would love to chase lizards. But Walter has told me stories about coyotes who live in the canyons and how they carry cats away. I would never take a chance with Minka.

Wolf opens his knapsack. He offers me fruit and cheese. I take an orange and a piece of cheddar.

"You have sad eyes, Tiger," he says. "A bright smile but sad eyes."

He waits for me to say something. I don't.

"You want to talk about it?" he asks.

"No."

"Okay."

We sit quietly for a moment.

"Maybe someday," I tell him. "Maybe someday I'll tell you about it."

"Okay," he says.

"But not today."

"Whenever," he says.

I nod.

That night I catch hell from Bitsy. She saw me riding back from the canyon and I wasn't wearing my helmet.

"I guess I forgot it," I say, sheepishly.

"Safety first, Davey," Bitsy says. "Just don't forget it again. We're trying to take good care of you but you've got to help us."

What does she mean by that? I can take care of myself. But I know that from now on I will have to be more careful or she won't let me ride the bicycle.

On the first Saturday in October we leave the house at six A.M. to drive down to Albuquerque to see the balloons take off at the annual hot air balloon festival. On the way, we stop at Dunkin' Donuts in Santa Fe and stuff ourselves on honey glazed crullers. Jason convinces Bitsy to buy him a box of Munchkins for the road.

We get to Albuquerque just before eight A.M. and line up with hundreds of other cars to watch as the balloons fill the sky with brilliant colors. Jason and I sit on the hood of the Blazer.

"Would you go up in one, Davey?" Jason asks.

"In a minute," I say.

"It's beautiful to watch," Bitsy says, "but only a fool would actually participate."

"Well, I'd do it," I tell her.

"Then so would I," Jason says.

"There's no point in arguing over whether you would or you wouldn't," Walter says. "It's a moot question."

"What's moot?" Jason asks.

"It means it doesn't matter because it isn't going to happen," Walter tells him.

"Oh," Jason says.

"I'd like to go up and never come down," Mom says.

We all look at her. What does she mean, never come down?

On the way home I promise myself that some day I will go up in a hot air balloon. I picture myself taking off. I wave at the crowd as it grows smaller and smaller, until the people watching are just tiny dots on the earth, while I am floating in my own world of sky and clouds and quiet.

By the time we get halfway home my mother has developed another headache, even worse than the last one. Bitsy tells her to close her eyes and try to sleep.

Jason babbles on about the balloons. He is full of questions about how they work.

Bitsy tells him that there are accidents almost every year. That something always goes wrong.

I read the paper carefully all week, and if anything has gone wrong with one of the balloons I can't find a story about it.

My mother has three more headaches in a row. She says they come on suddenly, like a blinding white light, piercing her eyes. After the third one Bitsy and Walter take her to their doctor, who recommends a specialist. The specialist believes that the headaches are caused by tension, by anxiety, by depression. He is sure that they are not your usual migraines, although the symptoms are the same.

One night I am sitting up in bed reading the current issue of *People* magazine. I had to buy it on the sly and sneak it up to my room. Walter considers it trash and wouldn't think of having a copy in his house. But I have seen Bitsy thumbing through it while waiting on line at the Safeway, so I'm not concerned when she knocks on my door. "Surprise," she says. She's carrying a tray with two graham crackers and a cup of cocoa. I feel about six years old, especially when I see the marshmallows floating on top.

She hands me the tray, then sits on the edge of my bed.

"Thanks," I say. "I was just thinking about how good a cup of cocoa would taste." Of course, I wasn't, but Bitsy believes me. I take a bite of graham cracker, then a sip of cocoa, wondering why Bitsy is sitting on my bed.

"Well . . ." she finally says. "I wanted to talk to you about your mother."

"What about her?" I ask.

"She's under a lot of stress."

"I know."

"And Walter and I don't think she should leave until she's feeling better."

I don't say anything so Bitsy continues.

"We feel responsible for you . . . we can't send you and Jason home with Gwen this way. She's in a daze. It's all beginning to hit her now. She needs time to mend. So we'd like you to stay a while longer."

Bitsy is explaining about my mother as if I am going to give her a hard time about going home. The truth is, Bitsy is right and I know it. We can't go home with Mom this way. Who would take care of her? What would I do when she gets one of her headaches?

"Jason is anxious to get back to school," Bitsy says, "so tomorrow I'm taking him over to Aspen. It's a very good elementary school. All of our schools are very good. Do you know we have more National Merit finalists than any other city in the country?"

"Jason likes to go to school," I say. "I think it's a good idea for him."

"And then I'll take you over to register at the high school."

I snap to attention and almost spill my cocoa. "I don't want to go to school here," I say.

"Why not? It's a very good school."

"That's not the point."

"Then what is?"

"I don't want to go to school this year. I'd rather take the year off."

"Oh, Davey . . . you can't do that."

"I don't see why not. I'll study at home. I'll learn astronomy. I can keep up . . . I know I can . . . I've thought it all out . . . and I'll help around the house and I'll babysit for Jason and . . ."

"You *have* to go to school," Bitsy says. "You've missed more than a month already."

I can tell that her mind is made up. That I have no choice. So much for my fantasy.

"How long do you think we'll be staying?" I ask.

"I can't tell you that."

"But I have to know. It's important."

"I don't know myself, Davey. It depends on your mother."

"But how can I go to school without knowing how long I'm going to stay?"

"What does that have to do with it?"

"Everything. I have to know if I should bother to make friends."

"Of course you should make friends," Bitsy says. "What kind of question is that?"

"It's an important question." But I can see that she has no idea what I am talking about. There is no point in trying to explain.

When Bitsy has gone back downstairs, I get out of bed and walk down the hall to say good-night to my mother. I open her door without knocking. She is sitting on the bed, surrounded by old photos. She is holding one of my father. She presses it to her face and says, "Oh, Adam . . . I miss you so much." She begins to weep quietly.

I close the door to her room. I don't want her to know I've seen her.

FIFTEEN

I have only three free days before school. I spend each of them in the canyon, with Wolf. He always has to leave before two o'clock. I figure he has a job. I don't ask him any questions, he doesn't ask me any. I like it that way.

Wolf tells me stories about the Anasazi, the Ancient Ones. They used to live in this canyon and in the canyons and cliffs all around here. He takes me for a walk and shows me a cliff dwelling. I try to imagine us hundreds of years ago. Tiger and Wolf, living in a cave together. We would make love on rocks that have been warmed by the sunshine. We would raise babies, fat and happy.

On the third day Wolf brings me a book. *The First Americans.* It is about the history of this area. "Thanks," I say. "I'll read it and bring it back next week."

"No, it's for you to keep," he says.

I open it. On the first page he has written *To Tiger Eyes, who makes me laugh. From Wolf.*

I look over at him.

"They are, you know," he says.

"What?"

"Your eyes. They remind me of a tiger's, the way they change color in the light, from golden to brown."

"When's the last time you saw a tiger?" I ask.

"I have a cat," he says. "That's close enough."

I laugh, wanting to hug him, wanting him to hug me. But he doesn't, and neither do I. "Thank you for the book," I say. "And for being my friend."

"It's good to have a friend," he says.

"Yes . . . I know."

On Monday morning Bitsy insists on accompanying me to Los Alamos High School. She asks me a hundred times if I need anything. I tell her I don't but she slips me ten dollars just in case.

"Walter and I want you to have an allowance while you're here. Of course, we'll expect you to help around the house but you've been very nice about doing that without being asked."

"Thanks," I say. I feel uncomfortable taking money from Bitsy and decide to discuss the situation with Mom.

At the high school we ask a boy with a calculator strapped to his belt where the office is, and then we take a wrong turn and miss it anyway. Bitsy stops a group of girls and asks again. I look away, as if I have nothing to do with any of this.

When we get to the office I want to register as a temporary student but I am told there is no such thing. They want my records from Atlantic

City, and a medical history from my doctor. I begin to explain that we don't have my school records because we thought we were here for a visit, when Bitsy produces them from her purse. I am surprised and confused. Bitsy says, "We sent for them . . . last week." I don't know whether to believe her or not.

I am told to have a seat, that a guidance counselor will be with me in a few minutes. Bitsy sits next to me. I don't want her hanging around. "I know you have a lot to do this morning," I say. I don't know that she has anything to do but I want to get rid of her. I want to do this on my own.

"I haven't got anything to do that can't wait," Bitsy says, smiling.

I sense that she is enjoying all of this. It's like a new game for her. Instant Motherhood. But I am not angry with her. My own mother is home in bed, zonked out on headache medicine. If I am angry at anyone this morning, it's Mom.

Finally, I convince Bitsy that it is okay for her to leave. I reassure her that I will be just fine, and reluctantly she stands up, then embarrasses me by kissing my cheek, as if she won't see me for a year. I breathe a sigh of relief when she is gone.

I am shown into the guidance counselor's office at last. We talk about what courses I should take. I tell him what I was taking in Atlantic City and he arranges a schedule for me here. English, something called American Cultures, Geometry, and French II.

"What about Science?" he asks, pulling on his ear lobe. "We try to encourage our sophomores to take Chemistry."

"I'd rather take Astronomy," I say. I am getting better and better at identifying stars, planets, and constellations.

"We don't offer Astronomy."

"Well then, I'll just skip a science course and take typing."

He looks up at me.

"I don't think I can handle Chemistry right now," I explain. Why should I kill myself with work? I think. I'm only going to be here for a little while. And the truth is, I'm not sure I'd be able to memorize all the symbols that go with Chemistry, especially after missing more than a month of school.

"All right," he says. He doesn't give me a hard time about it. He schedules me for typing instead.

I am late getting to my first period class, which is English. I hand my card to the teacher, who is a young guy wearing jeans and a sweater. His name is Mr. Vanderhoot. He reads my card out loud. "Davis Wexler."

"Davey," I tell him. "Everybody calls me Davey."

"Sure. Okay, Davey. Have a seat. Anywhere is

fine. We're reading Dickens' *Great Expectations.* Have you read it?"

"No."

"Good. You can pick up a copy after class. And get the notes from somebody smart. Let's see . . ." He looks around the room. "Try Jane. Jane, raise your hand. There she is," he says to me.

Mr. Vanderhoot seems flaky. I like him already.

After class Jane comes up to me. "That's why my parents named me Jane," she says.

"What?" I am confused.

"You know . . . that Davis-Davey business. With a simple name like Jane you never run into trouble."

"Oh, that," I say. "I'm used to it."

"You can take my notes home tonight. They're good."

"Thanks."

We discover that we both have second period free and we walk outside together. Jane is tall and blonde and she would be beautiful except for her chin, which is practically non-existent. We cross the parking lot, then the walking bridge over Diamond Drive, and go into a sleazy store, where Jane buys V-8 juice and pretzels. I don't like V-8 so I get a can of grapefruit juice instead.

Outside the store a group of boys wearing cowboy boots and ten gallon hats call lewd things to us. Jane ignores them and mutters, "Stomps."

We cross back over the walking bridge and sit on the grassy area in front of the high school. There is a cool breeze and Jane pulls her poncho around her while I zip up my jacket.

"Where're you from?" Jane asks, guzzling V-8 juice from the can.

"Atlantic City," I tell her.

"Where's that . . . California?" she asks.

"No, New Jersey."

"Oh, right . . . New Jersey."

"Yes," I say, amazed that she thought Atlantic City is in California.

"I guess I was thinking of Studio City. That's in California." She nibbles on a pretzel. "Atlantic City . . . that's where the Miss America pageant is held . . . right?"

"Right," I say.

"My sister was a state finalist one year but she lost out to this girl who could whistle Beethoven." Jane polishes off the rest of the pretzels, brushes the crumbs from her hands and says, "So you just moved up here?"

"Yes. A few weeks ago."

"Is your father a physicist?"

"No," I say. "My father's . . . dead." It is the first time I have said that to anyone.

"Oh," Jane says. "I'm sorry."

"He died over the summer," I tell her. "Of a heart attack." Once I get started I can't stop myself. "He died in his sleep. Everyone says it was a good way to go. That there was no pain. He was only thirty-four." Why am I doing this? Why am I telling her this story?

"I don't know what to say," Jane tells me. "It sounds terrible."

"My uncle's a physicist," I say. "We're living with him, and my aunt." I want to change the subject now. I want to get away from how my father died. "Where are you from?"

"Me . . . I'm from right here . . . Los Alamos."

"Really?"

"Yes. I was born here. I've never lived any place else. But I've been to Kansas. That's where my grandparents live, and I've been to Tennessee. My father worked at the lab there . . . at Oak Ridge . . . for six months. It's a lot like here." She smashes her V-8 can and tosses it up into the air, then catches it. A few drops of juice trickle out and land in her hair.

"Where're you living . . . White Rock or The Hill?"

"The Hill," I say. "The western area. How about you?"

"Bathtub Row," she tells me. "Look, I've got to run now. I've got another class. I'll meet you later and give you my notes, okay?"

"Sure. Okay."

• • •

At dinner I tell Bitsy and Walter about Jane. "She lives on Bathtub Row."

Jason laughs and spits milk out of his mouth and nose at the same time. "Is that near Toilet Terrace?" he asks. "Or Sink Street?"

Bitsy explains that Bathtub Row is the most prestigious area in town. The houses there are on the grounds of what used to be the exclusive Los Alamos boys school. In the old days, before Los Alamos became the Atomic City, the boys school was all that was up here. Then, in the 40's, when Oppenheimer and the other famous scientists gathered to develop the Bomb, the most important ones got to live in these houses, which were the only ones having bathtubs.

"Your friend must be the daughter of someone high up in the Lab, to live on Bathtub Row," Bitsy says. "What's her last name?"

"I don't know. I didn't ask."

After dinner Walter wants to see my course schedule. He hits the roof when he finds out that I am not taking a science course. "How could they let you register without insisting on a science course?"

"I wanted to take typing instead," I explain. "I can always take Chemistry next year."

"Typing," Walter says, angrily. "Ridiculous. And next year you should be taking Physics I. You're going to fall behind."

I feel like telling him that I have no intention of taking Physics I, not next year, and not ever.

"You have to think of your future," Walter tells me. "You want to get into a good college, don't you?"

"I don't know," I say.

"Of course you know."

"No, I don't! I don't even know if I want to go to college."

Walter pours himself a glass of brandy, sloshes it around in his glass, then takes a hearty drink. "What do you want to do with your life, Davey?" he asks.

"How do I know? I'm only fifteen!"

"It's never too soon to start planning," he calls, but I am already storming out of the room, with Minka at my heels.

I go straight to my mother's room, to tell her that Walter is a pain and I don't feel like discussing my life with him and she better do something about it, something to shut him up. But Mom is asleep, her mouth half open. Her breath sounds raspy. There are photos scattered across the bed. I feel so angry I want to shake her.

I go to my own room and flop down on my bed with a copy of *Great Expectations.*

I am on Chapter Two when Jason comes to my room. But I don't remember anything about Chapter One and I can't keep any of the characters straight.

"What's wrong with Mom?" Jason asks.

"You know," I tell him. "She has headaches."

He is wearing his football pajamas and looks very small and sweet. "Don't worry. She'll be okay."

"Maybe not," he says. "Maybe she's going to die."

"She's not going to die," I say.

"How do you know?"

"I just do."

"If she does die will we stay here, with Uncle Walter and Aunt Bitsy?"

"She's *not* going to die."

"But if she does . . ."

"Yes," I say, closing my book. "I suppose we'd stay here."

"That's all I wanted to know."

"Jason . . ." I say. He has a loose tooth and he wiggles it with his fingers. He is so innocent, I think.

"Yeah . . ."

"Aren't you going to kiss me goodnight?"

"Me . . . kiss you?"

"Yes. Come on . . ." I hold my arms out to him. "Pretend I'm not your sister. Pretend I'm some beautiful princess."

He comes closer to my bed and I reach out and hug him. "It's going to be all right," I whisper into his hair. "It is . . . it is . . . it is . . ."

SIXTEEN

On Saturday I ride to the canyon. There is a chill in the air and I wear my fisherman's sweater. When I look up into the mountains I see that the leaves of the aspen trees have turned color, making the whole mountainside a beautiful shade of gold against the deep blue of the sky. Tomorrow Walter and Bitsy are taking us for a drive into the mountains so that we can see the aspen up close.

I pedal hard and fast, anxious to reach the canyon.

Wolf is there, waiting for me. "Where've you been, Tiger?"

"School," I tell him. "They made me go to school."

"School," he repeats, nodding. He doesn't ask who made me go. He doesn't ask why I haven't gone until now.

We climb down into the canyon. I am able to climb much faster now. I have learned by watching and imitating Wolf. My hiking boots are comfortable on my feet, as if they belong there.

At the bottom we rest on a rock. "Remember the time you told me I have sad eyes?" I say.

"I remember."

"It's because my father's dead."

Wolf looks at me, shakes his head slowly, and says, "We have a lot in common, Tiger . . . because mine is dying."

Later, when it is time to leave the canyon I say, "I didn't make you laugh today."

And Wolf says, "I didn't feel like laughing."

I ride home feeling very sad. I wish I could talk to my mother. But when I get back she is sound asleep again, the shades in her room pulled down, making it as dark as night. Sometimes I feel she has vanished from my life. And I miss her.

A few days later Walter presents me with a small card. "Keep this in your wallet, Davey. Now that you're a member of this family there's a space reserved for you in a bomb shelter."

"A bomb shelter?" I say and I begin to laugh, half out of nervousness, half out of disbelief.

But Walter looks very serious and says, "Yes. The numbers are printed on the card. Try to memorize them."

"Are we going to have a war?" I ask. "Are we going to be bombed?"

"No," Walter says. "At least I hope not. But it's always better to be prepared. The problem with this country is we never act until it's too late. The Russians, on the other hand, have an outstanding civil defense program. If they're attacked, chances are, they'll survive. I wish I could say the same for us. It's just like the energy crisis. This country is waiting until the lights go out. Then we'll see how fast we accept nuclear energy. But by then it will be too late. Too late. Anyway, keep your card . . . chances are you'll never need it."

Walter is full of gloom tonight. And he is on his third glass of brandy.

SEVENTEEN

There are more than 250 clubs in this town and Bitsy belongs to nine of them, not counting morning walk, twice a week Jazzercise and batiking class. Her calendar is so full it looks like a doctor's appointment book. Still, she always has time for the family, especially Jason, who is growing closer and closer to her and Walter. One night I hear Bitsy telling Walter that Jason reminds her of Adam, when he was a boy. I think Bitsy misses my father more than she lets us know.

There are a lot of clubs and associations at the high school, too. Danielle, a girl in my American Cultures class, is trying to get me to join the Society for the Preservation of Creative Anachronisms. She dresses in a toga and medieval type sandals that lace up her legs. She wears a fuzzy, hobbit-like creature pinned to her shoulder. During class she knits. I've never seen her take a note, yet I know that she is a straight A student.

"We have jousting matches," she tells me on Wednesday after class. She stands so close I can smell the garlic on her breath.

I have no idea what creative anachronisms are

or why anyone would want to preserve them. But I say, "Look . . . I'm not really into jousting."

She shakes her head, clearly disappointed, and drops an arm around my shoulder. "You could give it a try."

I inch away, wondering if she is gay. "I'm overextended now," I tell her. This is an expression I have picked up from Bitsy, who uses it on the phone whenever she is asked to volunteer for this or that community activity.

"How so?" Danielle asks, fingering the fuzzy creature on her shoulder as if it is alive. She is not one to give up easily.

"I've got a lot of family responsibilities," I tell her. I don't know why I am bothering to make excuses since I don't owe her an explanation.

"Go on . . ." she says.

"And I'm a candy striper at the hospital." This is not exactly true, but Jane has been after me to join with her and now, on the spot, I decide that I will. Anything to get rid of Danielle.

Danielle accepts this piece of information with a shrug. "I thought you were the unusual type," she says, pulling a green cape around her shoulders. "But I see that I was wrong." She swoops past me and out the door.

I have learned plenty about the dynamics of this school in just two weeks. For one thing, everyone is classified by groups. There are Coneheads, Loadies, Jocks, and Stomps.

Coneheads are into computers and wear calculators strapped to their belts. They are carbon copies of their fathers, grinding away for the best grades so that they can go to the best colleges. Loadies are into booze and drugs and there is plenty available. You can buy whatever you want out of the trunk of a car in the parking lot. Jocks are jocks. Every group makes fun of every other group. Coneheads laugh at Jocks. Jocks laugh at Loadies. Loadies laugh at Stomps. Stomps dress in ten gallon hats and cowboy boots. They chew tobacco and spit and ride around in pickup trucks, looking for fights.

I know that I will never fit in here. Of course, there are other kids like me, other kids who don't fit in either. There is a girl, Ann, who screams in the hallways. I can't figure her out. Maybe she realizes the futility of trying to fit in, just as I do.

There are guys who aren't really Coneheads, but who aren't anything else either. And it's tough on them. Because the kids here are very into putting down anybody and anything that is not exactly like they are. I sometimes think it would be terrific if all of us who don't fit in formed a group called the Left-overs. Then we could get together and laugh our heads off at the Stomps, Loadies, Jocks and Coneheads.

There are only one or two blacks in the school and one night I ask Walter how come.

"To tell the truth, Davey," he says, "there are

very few black scientists in this country. We're trying to recruit more. We're trying to encourage bright black boys and girls to get into science. There are scholarships available."

"My friend, Lenaya, wants to be a scientist," I remind him.

"Yes, I know."

But it's not only blacks who are missing. In New Mexico there are three cultures: Hispanic, Anglo, and Native American. When I was in third grade we studied Native Americans, except we called them Indians. And what we learned about them then, embarrasses me now.

My family is Anglo. White. Caucasian. And we are in the minority in this state. But not in Los Alamos. Los Alamos is an Anglo town. Absolutely. And in our high school there are no Native Americans and there are only a handful of Hispanic kids, who happen to live here because their fathers work at the Lab, doing maintenance.

I head for my Geometry class but the teacher doesn't show. This isn't unusual. He has missed five classes since I came to school. And we've never had a substitute which means he isn't absent for the day, but just for our class. When he doesn't show he arranges for us to see a film, usually having nothing to do with math. Most kids settle back and go to sleep. Someone almost always snores. A couple of kids use the darkened room to make out. But I don't mind the films. I find them more interesting than geometry.

Today's film is about hemophilia. The narrator has a deep voice and says, *Hemophilia is a hereditary plasma-coagulation disorder, principally affecting males but transmitted by females and characterized by excessive, sometimes spontaneous bleeding.* I already know this because in eighth grade I read *Nicholas and Alexandra.* Still, I am not prepared to deal with a film on bleeding. My heart starts to pound and I can't catch my breath. Halfway through the film I have to leave the room, afraid that I am going to pass out.

Reuben, who is somewhere between a Conehead and a regular person, comes out into the hall after me. He is in three of my classes and I have caught him watching me since the first day I came to this school. This is the first time he has spoken to me. "Can't stand the sight of blood, huh?" he jokes.

I know that he means well but as soon as he says it I feel a wave of nausea and am sure I am going to throw up. I press my head against the cool concrete wall of the corridor and count slowly to twenty. The nausea passes.

"You want some water?" Reuben asks.

"No."

"What can I do?"

"Nothing," I say. "Go back to class."

"What about you?"

"I'm going home." And I walk right out of school. No permission. No excuses. I just take off and walk home.

When I get there the house is quiet. Bitsy is at the museum, giving her tour. *And this is the bomb that we dropped on Nagasaki . . . and this is the bomb that we dropped on Hiroshima . . .*

I go upstairs, passing my mother's room. I look in and see her sprawled across the bed. She is holding a couple of photos.

"Mom," I say, "what are you doing?"

She looks at me as if she doesn't know who I am.

"You have to stop taking that headache medicine," I tell her. "Do you hear me . . . you have to stop!"

She nods. "Yes," she says. "I have to stop."

I get this feeling that my mother and I have changed places and I don't like it. That she is the little girl and I am the mother. I don't want this kind of responsibility laid on me and I am glad that Walter and Bitsy are around.

Yet I remember that when I fell apart and wouldn't get out of bed, Mom was there, to help me get back on my feet. And something inside of me tells me that I shouldn't be angry at her now. That I should be helping. But I don't know what to do.

It is more than the headache medicine though, more than the headaches themselves, and this time, when Bitsy takes Mom to the doctor, he recommends therapy. He sets up an appointment at the family counseling center for Mom. She is to see someone named Miriam Olnick tomorrow afternoon.

"I have to get myself together," Mom explains that night at the dinner table. It is the first time in a week that she is joining us for dinner.

Jason taps his fork against the table, as if he is keeping time to some marching tune in his head.

"I have to get myself together," Mom says again.

Walter reaches over and covers Jason's hand with his, silencing the fork.

"I'm not myself," Mom says. "I'm not the person I used to be before Adam . . ." Her voice trails off and there is a heavy silence at the table. It is the first time she has said his name out loud in front of us. "Before Adam . . ." She tries again, but her voice breaks.

"Died," I say.

Everyone looks at me. I feel my cheeks flush. Then everyone looks away as if I have broken some deep, dark secret. Jason goes back to tapping his fork against the table.

"Well . . ." Bitsy finally says, trying to sound cheerful, "you know how quickly food cools off in the high altitude . . ." and she serves each of us a healthy portion of chicken tetrazzini.

EIGHTEEN

I tell Jane that I have decided to join candy stripers with her.

She says, "Terrific . . . it'll look really good on our college applications."

I think about explaining that that's not the reason I'm joining. That college is about the farthest thing from my mind right now. That I don't even know if I *want* to go to college. But I decide to say nothing. I don't feel like getting into another hassle over my future.

We walk to the Los Alamos Medical Center together. We go to a room marked Director of Volunteers where we listen to a lecture on the duties of all after school helpers. There are about fifteen of us, and three are boys. I try to picture them dressed in candy-striped jumpers and I begin to giggle. Once I get started I can't stop. Jane looks over at me and raises her eyebrows. I look away and try to control myself.

"Basically," the director says, "your duties are to assist the nurses and the aides. You'll be delivering mail and flowers, making sure that the patients have fresh water, and helping to serve the evening meal. You may not, under any circumstances, administer medication to the patients, nor can you bring them anything to eat or drink except what has been ordered for them. Occasionally, one of our volunteers runs into a troublesome patient. If that happens, report directly to me."

Jane leans over and whispers, "When my sister was a candy striper she had a patient who flashed her."

I mouth the word *gross* at Jane, then go back to listening to the director.

"We certainly appreciate your time and assistance," she says. "And now, if you'll come with me, we'll see about your uniforms and you can get to work."

I don't have to worry about the boys walking around in jumpers after all. They are issued white shirts and candystriped ties.

My first job is pushing the water cart down the hall, stopping at each room and filling the patients' pitchers with fresh water and ice.

I go into a semi-private room. There are flowers all over the place. Both patients are middle-aged women and neither one looks especially sick. They are sitting up in their beds, reading—one, a Harold Robbins novel; the other, *Atlantic Monthly*. They barely glance my way as I fill their water pitchers.

The next room is also a semi-private but there is just one patient. An older man. He is bald, very thin, and his skin is a grayish color.

"Hello," he says. "I've been waiting for you."

He speaks in a lyrical New Mexican accent. I've been listening to the Spanish radio station in my room at night. I love the sound of the language, even though I don't understand a word. And the same musical sound carries through to the Hispanic's English.

"You've been waiting for me?" I say.

"For any pretty girl."

Oh oh, I think, remembering Jane's story about her sister and the flasher. If he tries anything funny I will just tell him *to put it away* and I will go directly to the volunteers' office.

I fill his water pitcher and when my back is turned he says, "Look at this."

I spin around, almost dropping the pitcher, and see him winding up a toy. It is a dancing bear. He places it on his bedside table and the bear dances around in a circle. "My son brought it to me . . . from California . . . he goes to school there."

I laugh nervously, partly at the dancing bear, and partly at myself, for having been so suspicious.

"Does your father work at the Lab?" he asks.

"No, but my uncle does," I tell him.

"I'm on the maintenance crew fifteen years." He holds out his hand, to shake mine, and introduces himself. "Willie Ortiz."

His hand is boney and fragile and when I shake it I can't help noticing the difference between mine and his. "I'm Davey Wexler," I tell him.

He winds up the dancing bear again and this time my laugh is genuine. "That's so cute."

"You like it? It's yours." And he holds it out to me before it has wound down, so that the bear's legs are still moving.

"Oh no," I say, "I can't."

"Why not?"

"Because . . ." I begin. "Because it's yours."

"Hijole! You're a tough one. I tell you what. I'm not going to be here for long and when I'm gone I want you to have it. Okay?"

"Sure okay . . ."

"It's cancer, you know . . . but I'm ready to die."

He says it so easily I am sure I have misunderstood.

"For a long time," he says. "Too long. In and out of the hospital. But this is the end."

I turn away and look out the window. The sun is setting. I have never seen anything like a New Mexican sunset. The whole sky turns pink, then red, then purple. Why did he have to tell me he is dying?

"Don't be sad," he says.

I face him again, hoping he won't see how close to tears I am.

"Well . . ." I say, "I'll see you next week?"

"Sure. Next week."

After work, I meet Jane outside. It is growing

cold and dark. I button my jacket and turn up the collar. I'm going to have to buy a hat and gloves.

"How did it go?" Jane asks.

"Okay."

"Any trouble?"

"No. You?"

"Nothing."

We begin to walk home.

"If you had your choice," I say, "Would you rather die slowly, of cancer, or fast, like being shot?"

"I'm not sure," Jane says. "With the cancer you'd have time to get ready. And you'd feel so sick you'd probably want it to be over. If you got shot, well, it'd be so sudden . . ."

I don't wait for her to finish. I interrupt with, "You wouldn't have time to say goodbye."

NINETEEN

Bitsy is reading a book called *How to Feed Your Kids Right*. And now, every morning, Jason and I get a teaspoon of raw bran in our cereal. This will prevent hemorrhoids in later life, Bitsy assures us.

"What's a hemorrhoid?" Jason asks.

"Never mind," Bitsy says. "Just eat your cereal with bran and you'll never have to know."

"But if I don't know what it is how do I know I don't want it."

"Believe me," Bitsy says. "You don't."

Bitsy is taking us very seriously, as if we are her kids, as if we are her responsibility. But I figure we'll be going home soon. Maybe before Christmas, because Mom has seen Miriam Olnick at the family counseling center four times in the past two weeks. She has joined Bitsy's Jazzercise class and is looking healthier. She is still tense and apt to run off to her room when you least expect it, but she's getting better. Although sometimes when I am trying to talk to her, like about Bitsy giving me an allowance, she spaces out and I know she's not hearing a word I say.

"What do you and Miriam talk about?" I ask

one evening. I am sitting on the kitchen counter, nibbling a piece of celery and Mom is fixing her specialty, spinach pie. She has volunteered to make dinner tonight, to give Bitsy a break, but I don't think Bitsy is overjoyed. She considers the kitchen her turf. This is the first time that Mom has cooked a meal since we got to Los Alamos.

"We talk about everything," Mom says. "It's easy to talk to her."

"Do you talk about Dad?" I ask. "About that night?"

Mom hesitates, then says, "Yes." She says it very quietly and she doesn't look up.

How come she can talk about him to Miriam, but not to me?

When dinner is ready I help Mom serve it. Walter just picks at the spinach pie and I feel angry at him for making Mom think there is something wrong with it.

He makes things even worse by saying, "It's good, Gwen. It's just that I had a big lunch."

"It's outstanding," Bitsy says. "I haven't had spinach pie for years. Walter doesn't like . . ." She stops abruptly and covers her mouth with her hand, realizing her mistake.

"I guess you could say I'm strictly a meat and potatoes man," Walter explains.

"It's all right," Mom says. "I should have asked before I made it."

I am hoping that Mom doesn't break down

and cry over this. She sounds as if she is on the brink. I wish we could just laugh it off, but there is too much tension at the table for laughing. I can't help remembering that we had spinach pie on the night that my father died . . .

We'd been walking on the beach—all four of us—singing *This Old Man* at the top of our lungs. Mom and Dad had their arms around each other and were in one of their touchy-feely moods. I was thinking about later, about going out with Hugh, when Jason came up from behind and dumped a pail of water over my head. With his Dracula cape flying behind him, he ran away yelling, "Can't catch me . . . can't catch me . . ." And then we went home for supper. Spinach pie, a green salad and sourdough bread . . .

I wonder if Jason remembers that, too. I look over at him. He is shoveling in his food.

"So what's new in school, Jase?" I ask.

"My teacher's so tall she can open the windows without a pole."

"Wow . . . that tall, huh?"

"And smart too," Jason says. "She knows everything."

"She sounds great," I tell him.

"I told you we had excellent schools here," Bitsy says.

* * *

The next night, I am lying on the living room floor, playing Monopoly with Jason. Jason lands on Virginia Avenue and even though I already own St. Charles Place and State Street, he buys it. He never misses a chance to buy Virginia Avenue because that's where we live in Atlantic City. Playing Monopoly reminds me of home.

Walter and Bitsy are taking Mom to a party tonight. Mom comes downstairs wearing her long skirt and a black sweater. She looks nice and I tell her so.

"Thanks, honey," she says.

"And you smell good, too," Jason says, as she kisses him goodnight.

"It's Chanel Number Five. I bought it today."

I roll the dice, move my man eight spaces and land on *Go to Jail.*

"Too bad!" Jason says, holding up his *Get Out of Jail Free* card.

Walter helps Bitsy, and then Mom, into their coats. Mom says, "The police and fire department numbers are on the bulletin board in the kitchen. And so is the number at the Grants', where we're going. If there's any trouble just call us there."

"Hey, Mom . . ." I say, "I used to babysit all the time in Atlantic City . . . remember? I know what to do."

Mom looks doubtful and turns to Bitsy. "I don't know . . . maybe I should stay home tonight. I'm not really feeling up to a party."

•

"Nonsense," Walter says. "It will do you good."

"Don't let anyone in," Mom says to me. "I don't care who they say it is . . . I don't care if they say it's the police . . . don't open the door for anyone."

"It's all right, Gwen," Bitsy says. "There's no place safer than The Hill, believe me."

I realize suddenly what this is all about. Tonight is the first time Mom is leaving us alone at night. The first time since my father was killed.

I hear the front door close.

"Okay," Jason says, "I'm building a hotel on Boardwalk and another one on Park Place, and two houses on . . ."

"Have you been stealing from the bank, you little creep?"

Jason has trouble keeping a straight face. "Who, me?"

I know that he has. That while I was talking with Mom, he was helping himself to five-hundred-dollar bills.

I let out a whoop and Jason takes off, racing through the house. I chase him and we both laugh our heads off. When I finally catch him, I pin him down and begin to tickle him.

"No . . . please . . . stop . . . stop . . ." Jason screams.

I stop, but I don't let him up.

We are both out of breath and panting.

After a while I say, "Jason . . . do you miss Daddy?"

Jason turns his head to the side.

"Do you?"

He mashes his lips together and doesn't answer me.

"I know you do, Jason, so why don't you ever say it? And why don't you ever cry?"

"Crying is for babies," he mumbles.

"No," I tell him, "it's for everyone. When you feel sad it's okay to cry."

"Let me up," he says.

"Not until you say it. Not until you say you miss Daddy."

"No!" He struggles to get away from me.

"Okay," I tell him, "then I'll say it for you. I miss Daddy. I miss him a lot." I move aside then and Jason gets up and runs away from me.

"Jason . . ." I call, "don't you want to finish our game?"

But he is already upstairs. "Finish it yourself," he calls back, and he is crying.

I don't know why I did that. I don't know why I spoiled our game, our evening together. It's just that I have this need to talk about my father, with someone who knew him and loved him the way I did.

TWENTY

Jane phones and invites me to sleep over on Saturday night. "Come early," she says, "so we can spend the afternoon together."

Bitsy is impressed when she hears that I am going to spend the night at the Albertsons' house. "You know that Bud Albertson is a division leader and a very important part of the policy making group at the Lab. There are those who say that Bud has more clout than the director."

"I didn't know," I say. I do not add that I don't care.

"And Brenda is in my Thursday night group."

Bitsy's Thursday night group reads and discusses current books. This week it is a biography of Georgia O'Keefe.

I pack a small bag and walk over to Jane's house. It is my first visit to Bathtub Row. When I get there her brother-in-law, Howard, is in the driveway, waxing a pair of skis. I have never seen Howard but Jane has described her whole family to me. Howard is tall and thin and trying to grow a beard. Jane's sister is the first person he ever had sex with, and that was after they were married. I know a lot about Jane's family. I know that her parents make love once a week, on Saturday nights.

"Hello," Howard says to me. "You must be Davey."

"Yes."

"Jane's inside."

The house looks like a log cabin. It is set back from the road and surrounded by piñon pine and blue spruce trees. I knock on the front door and Jane lets me in.

"Hi," she says. "Come and meet my mom."

Inside, the house looks like a regular house, except for the logs showing through on one of the living room walls, giving it a rustic look.

I follow Jane to the kitchen where she introduces me to her mother, Brenda, who is chubby and dimpled, with a face like Jane's. She is baking cookies. Bitsy does a lot of baking too. Jason has become her apprentice. Together they bake chocolate chips, lemon-iced, sugar coated, oatmeal, applesauce, pinwheel—you name it, they bake it. I have this fantasy that Jason will get so good at baking cookies that when we go back to Atlantic City we'll open a cookie shop on the boardwalk. A really classy place. And we'll call it *Jason Wexler, Cookie Specialist,* or something like that. I'll do the publicity and Mom will take care of the business side of things. We'll make a fortune. All the big hotels will have branches of our shop. And we'll ship all over the world, just like James' Saltwater Taffy shops. We'll live in a penthouse apartment in one of the new hotels, with a view of the ocean from every room.

"Hello, dear," Jane's mother says. "I'm so glad to meet you."

There is a fat, beautiful baby crawling around on the kitchen floor. Jane scoops him up and plants a juicy kiss on his face. "And this is my nephew, Robby. Isn't he adorable?"

Jane passes him to me and he grabs a fistful of my hair and tries to chew on it. We all laugh as he babbles to us in baby talk.

Robby belongs to Howard, who was in the driveway, and to Linda, Jane's sister. She is the one who was once a finalist in the Miss New Mexico contest.

Jane's other sister, Taffy, is in business school in Albuquerque. She comes home every other weekend.

"Where's your father?" I ask Jane, as we walk through the house.

"In his study," Jane whispers, pointing to a closed door. "He's thinking. He always thinks on Saturdays. But you'll meet him later. He usually comes out to dinner. Come on upstairs . . . my room is a mess . . . I'm in the middle of cleaning out my closet."

I follow Jane up the stairs, admiring the polished wooden banister which feels cool and sleek under my hand.

"My mother is president of the Women's Hiking Association," Jane says, over her shoulder. "She knows the name of every wildflower in the Southwest."

"That's nice," I say.

Jane wasn't kidding about her room. It's a mess, with clothes scattered all over the place.

"I told you," she says, laughing.

"Where's the bathtub?" I ask.

"You want to take a bath . . . now?"

"No," I say, and I start to laugh too. "I want to see it for historical reasons."

"Oh, that," she says. "Come on." She takes my hand and leads me down a hallway, and into the bathroom. "Violà," she says.

The tub is old fashioned. It stands off the floor, on feet, and has separate faucets for hot and cold water. I look around for a sign that says *J. Robert Oppenheimer Bathed Here,* but I don't see one. New Jersey is full of signs proclaiming *George Washington Slept Here.*

I try to picture Oppenheimer sitting in the tub. Maybe he got his ideas while he was soaking or maybe he sailed plastic boats, like Jason does. Who knows?

We go back to Jane's room and I flop down on her bed. She turns on the radio. An old Eagles song is playing. She begins to fold her clothes and put them away.

I hum along with the radio and look around Jane's room. She has three posters taped to her wall. One of Jimmy McNicol, one of Eric Heiden on skates, and one of Bjorn Borg. They are all covered with lipstick kisses.

"It's how I blot my lipstick," Jane explains, when she sees me studying them.

I understand. I used to practice kissing on my pillow. But I don't tell this to Jane. Instead I say, "You hardly ever wear lipstick."

"I used to," she says. "I was really into makeup in ninth grade."

I'm surprised. Jane doesn't seem the type to experiment with makeup. But then I remember that Lenaya and I used to go to Woolworth's and try out all the samples on the counter when we were in eighth grade.

When Jane has finished putting away her clothes and the room looks reasonably neat, she takes out a Revlon nail-care kit and begins to give herself a manicure.

"Where do you want to go to college?" she asks, as she files her nails.

"I don't know," I say. "It's not as if we're seniors and have to decide right away."

"But it's something you have to plan for early."

"I don't even know if I want to go," I tell her.

"Really?"

"Yes. And I think it's stupid to worry about it so far in advance. You never know what's going to happen between now and then."

"I never thought of it that way," Jane says.

"My father wants me to go to MIT because that's where he went and my mother is talking up Wellesley because that's where she went. My parents expect a lot of me." She is painting her nails a pale peach color. "Linda and Taffy were big disappointments, especially to my father. Neither one of them ever did much in school. So it's all up to me."

"Nobody's going to tell me what to do with my life," I say.

"You're braver than I am."

"It doesn't have anything to do with being brave."

"I think it does." When her nails are polished to perfection she holds them up, admiring her work. "Want me to do yours?" she asks, as she blows on her own.

I look at my fingernails. They're a mess. I haven't paid any attention to them since last August. I used to keep them clipped short. But now they are all different lengths and ragged at the tips.

"You could use a good manicure," Jane says. "No offense, but I've noticed."

I nod and agree to let her do my nails. She shapes them with an emery board. Her touch is light.

The phone rings in the hall before Jane has finished filing the nails on my left hand. She rushes out to answer it. I pick up a copy of *Seventeen* and browse through it. The models are all perfect. I wish some of them had zits, or oily hair. I go to the mirror and examine my face. It is not one of my better days. I look tired and my hair is limp.

When Jane comes back her face is flushed and she says, "That was Ted."

Ted hangs out with Reuben, the guy who is always looking at me. I have suspected for weeks that Jane has a thing for Ted. This confirms it.

"He wants to come over tonight," she says, excitedly, ". . . with Reuben." She pauses and looks at me. "I said it would be okay."

Jane sits down and reaches for my hand. I hold it out and she continues to file my nails.

"If it's not okay with you I can call him back and tell him to make it another time."

Sometimes Jane is so polite it gets to me.

"We'll just take a walk or something," she says. "No big deal. I thought it would be okay with you. Otherwise I wouldn't have said *yes.*"

I can't bring myself to say that it is okay and I don't know why.

Jane has filed my pinky nail down to nothing. "Look," she says, her eyes wide, "just forget it. I'll go call him and make up some excuse."

"No," I finally manage. "It's okay. I don't mind."

She looks relieved. "It's not as if you hate him," she says.

"Right. I don't hate him."

Jane holds up a bottle of nail polish. "How

about this one?" she asks. "I think it'll look really good on you . . . with your coloring." She begins to paint my fingernails and the color, which looked almost brown in the bottle, turns out to be a putrid shade of purple.

"Do you have a lot of experience?" she asks.

"In what?" I say, thinking she is talking about my fingernails.

"You know . . . with boys."

"Oh, boys."

"Do you?"

"Not much," I tell her.

"How much?"

"Some."

"I don't have any," she says. "I've kissed two boys and that's it."

"Don't worry about it," I say.

"Don't worry about it?" she repeats. "What else is there to worry about . . . not counting school?"

Sometimes Jane seems so innocent I can't believe we are the same age.

"You know how I found out about sex?" she asks.

"No, how?"

"I looked it up in the card catalogue, in the library."

I laugh. "Really?"

"Really. You'd think that with two older sisters someone would have given me the facts, but when I asked them they said, 'Go ask Mother.'

And when I asked my mother she said, 'You're too young to be asking about that.' You'd think that they'd give us sex education in school, wouldn't you? I mean, it's all in the best interest of science."

Now we both laugh.

"So how far *have* you gone?" Jane asks.

I don't answer her. Instead, I examine my nails and say, "Thanks. They look nice." Then I blow on them, the way Jane did hers, to help them dry faster.

"All the way?" Jane says.

I realize that because I avoided the answer to her question she thinks I have a lot of experience. I try to set the record straight. "No," I say, emphatically. "Not all the way."

"Close?" she asks.

"No. Not even close." I don't tell her about Hugh. I don't tell her about the hot, sweaty summer nights. About the salty taste of his lips. About his body pressed against mine. That is not for sharing. Not with Jane. Not with anyone.

Before dinner I take a bath in the famous tub. I soak for a long time. My hair fans out in the water, which comes up to my chin. Usually, I try not to think about Hugh and how it was with us, because then I get all worked up and I don't want to deal with any of those feelings now. But I do remember. I remember everything. Especially the last night . . .

* * *

"So what's new, Davina?" Hugh asked. He knew my real name but called me Davina as a joke.

"Not much," I said.

We were sitting on the railing, overlooking the beach, eating soft ice cream cones. We'd already cruised the Boards in a motorized wicker chair and now it was dark. I clicked my feet together and one of my flip-flops fell off and landed on the sand. Hugh jumped down to retrieve it. As he put it back on my foot he caressed the inside of my leg. "How about a walk on the beach, Davina?"

"Come on, Hugh . . . you know I can't."

"I can't . . . I can't . . ." he said, mimicking me.

"You know it's a rule."

"And rules are made to be broken, right?"

"Not this one," I said. "But you can come back to our place."

"Your father will be there."

"So? There's always the backyard."

It wasn't that I didn't want to take a walk on the beach with Hugh. I did. I loved the idea of the moonlight on the ocean, the sand beneath our feet, of being alone, really alone, with him. But I'd promised my parents that I wouldn't.

So Hugh and I walked home and went directly to the small yard behind the store. I leaned back against the willow tree. The single light from the store cast a shadow on the scrubby grass. Hugh's arms were around me, his lips on my face, my neck. His breath was hot. I clutched his damp T-shirt as he slid his hand from my shoulder to the top of my halter, to my waist, and then back up again. The smell of my *Charlie* was in the air.

From the store we could hear a symphony playing on my father's radio. We were both breathing hard. Hugh's body was pressed against mine and he whispered, "Davey . . . oh, Davey . . ."

My knees were so weak I wanted to lie down. To lie down in Hugh's arms and let whatever might happen, happen. Whatever . . .

But then we heard a firecracker, and another, and another and another. Hugh pulled away from me, saying, "What the hell . . ."

Then both of us were running, running toward the store.

TWENTY-ONE

"Davey . . . are you almost done?" Jane calls, knocking on the bathroom door. "Dinner's ready."

"Be right out," I call back, swallowing the sob that was working its way up into my throat. I splash my face, step out of the tub, and dry off.

Downstairs, everyone is seated around the dinner table. They are waiting for us. "Sorry," I say. "I didn't know it was so late."

"That's all right, dear," Jane's mother says.

Jane's father is at the head of the table. He is a big man, with jowly cheeks, steel rimmed glasses, and gray wiry hair that is cut short. I notice the scar across his forehead. Jane told me that a year ago he was in a serious auto accident. I try not to stare at him as I take my seat. He says, "Hello, Davey." Then he and Howard engage in a lengthy conversation about the Lab. I don't even try to follow what they are talking about.

Robby sits in a high chair next to Linda and she feeds him bits and pieces from the table. I see that Linda is pregnant again and wonder why Jane hasn't told me.

The conversation at our end of the table centers around skiing. Linda and Jane both hope that it will snow early so that the ski area will be open before Christmas.

"Do you ski, Davey?" Jane's mother asks.

"No, but I'd like to learn."

"I don't either," she says, "but Dr. Albertson is an outstanding skier and all three girls have followed in his footsteps."

At first I'm not sure who Dr. Albertson is. Then I realize it is Jane's father. I tend to think of the word *doctor* as meaning medical doctor or even dentist, but Los Alamos is full of Ph.D.'s who call each other *doctor*.

"And don't forget Howard," Linda says. "Howard's a fantastic skier. He practically grew up on skis. He's from Canada."

I wonder if Linda will ski this winter even though she is pregnant. I decide not to ask. Maybe she isn't pregnant after all. Maybe she's just fat.

"Robby's going to learn as soon as he's three," Linda says, giving him another bread crust.

We have chocolate cake and vanilla ice cream for dessert and when we are finished Jane's father stands and says, "Very nice, Brenda." Then he disappears into his study and the rest of us do the dishes.

At eight-thirty Ted and Reuben ring the bell. Jane lets them in. They wait in the entrance foyer rubbing their hands together. Their breath is smoky. We get our jackets and then the four of us take off, with Jane's mother calling, "Button up . . . it's very cold."

Outside, Ted reaches behind a tree and comes up with a bottle of vodka. "Didn't think it was wise to carry it into the house."

"Good thinking," Jane says.

Ted opens the bottle and as we walk along it is passed back and forth. I am not into booze and take only one swig. It burns going down my throat and then again as it hits my stomach. Reuben takes a couple of swallows and says, "Can't stand the stuff but it does warm you up."

I keep my hands in my pockets. I have the feeling that if I don't, Reuben will want to hold hands. It's not that I don't like him. I think he's okay. But I don't want him touching me.

Ted has his arm around Jane and they are drinking from the bottle and nuzzling each other. The next time Ted offers the bottle to us, Reuben shakes his head and says we've had enough.

There is no place to walk, except to town, and there is nothing open there, except the Pizza Hut and the movie. But the movie began at eight-fifteen. Besides, I saw it two years ago and it was a bore. The boys are starving so we go into the Pizza Hut and choose a booth near the back. The boys count their money. Between them they have eight dollars and sixty-four cents. They decide to split a medium pizza with extra cheese and sausage. We order a pitcher of Cokes and after the waitress brings it, Ted takes the bottle of vodka out of his jacket pocket and pours a couple of shots into his Coke and then, into Jane's.

Jane's face is red and she is laughing and slobbering all over the place. I don't like to see my friends drunk. Lenaya once said that if I drank myself I wouldn't feel so uncomfortable. But I don't like the way I feel when I drink, and I don't like the way I feel after, either. I once drank beer until I got sick and I hated it.

When we go back outside Jane begins to sing and she spins around and around in the parking lot, her arms open wide, like a whirling dervish. I can't believe that this is my friend, Jane, who seems shy and innocent and scared of the world.

"It's freezing," Ted says. "Let's warm up in a car."

"What car?" I ask.

"Any car," Ted says, looking around the parking lot. "They're all at the movies. They won't be out until ten-thirty." He goes from car to car, trying the doors, and on the fifth try he finds one that opens. It is a blue, four-wheel drive Subaru. Ted and Jane climb into the back seat, leaving the front for Reuben and me. I don't like this. The owner of the car could appear at any minute and then what? We could be arrested and our parents would be called. I'd never hear the end of it from Walter and Bitsy.

"Can't wait to take Driver's Ed," Reuben says. "Hitching around town is such a bitch. I live way out on Barranca." He rubs his hands together. "Wish we had the key to the ignition . . . at least we could have a little heat."

"Make your own," Ted calls from the back seat. He and Jane laugh hysterically, then Ted rolls down the window and tosses the empty bottle of vodka into the parking lot. We hear the sound of the glass smashing.

Jane and Ted are making out. I am aware of every grunt, every sigh, and I can't help thinking that for someone without experience Jane doesn't seem to be having much trouble.

Reuben and I sit like zombies, frozen to our seats, and not just because it is cold. We stare straight ahead, not talking, not touching, not even glancing at each other. I know that he wishes he could be some place else, just like I do. We are both uncomfortable but don't know how to get out of the situation. I try to block the sounds from the back seat by thinking of the canyon. But then Jane whimpers, "I'm not feeling very well . . . I'm feeling kind of . . . kind of . . ."

"Let her out . . . let her out . . ." Ted calls nervously, and both Reuben and I open our doors. Jane gets out just in time. She throws up all over the rear end of the Subaru.

Reuben and I are relieved. For the first time we look at each other and smile. Now we have an excuse to go home. But Jane is really out of it and we have to half-carry, half-drag her there. When we get to her house I say goodnight to the boys. I am feeling much friendlier toward Reuben now, especially since he didn't try anything in the car.

"See you Monday," he says to me.

"Right . . . Monday," I say.

Howard's car is gone and the front door is unlocked. I push it open slowly. I am a wreck trying to think of what I will say to Jane's parents. I rehearse a speech in my mind. *Jane isn't feeling too well,* I'll explain. *She ate a pizza downtown and it was just too much for her after your wonderful dinner, Mrs. Albertson. Actually, she got sick in the parking lot. Of course, it could be that she's coming down with the flu. There's a lot of it going around in school.*

Suppose her mother smells the booze and says, *You're a liar, Davey Wexler. And you're a bad influence on our little girl. We never should have let her invite you to spend the night.*

The house is very quiet. I hold my breath and somehow I manage to get Jane upstairs, and into her room, without her parents knowing. I remember that it is Saturday night. Jane's mother and father are probably locked into their bedroom, making love. Or maybe they did it while we were out and now they're sleeping. I don't want to think about sex anymore. It was bad enough listening to Ted and Jane.

I get Jane undressed down to her shirt and her underpants, pull the covers up around her, then climb into the bedroll her mother has set out for me. I fall asleep quickly and dream about Wolf. About the two of us together in our cave.

It is not the first time I have dreamed about him.

TWENTY-TWO

The next morning, at seven-thirty, there is a knock on our door. "Rise and shine," Jane's mother calls. "Breakfast is ready. We have to be at church before nine."

Jane rolls over, moans, then sits up and says, "Oh, my God . . . it's Sunday." She holds her hands to her head. "I feel terrible. I think I'm dying. Or did I die last night? What happened?"

"You don't remember?" I say.

"I remember the Pizza Hut . . . and drinking all that vodka . . ."

"And the car . . . you remember the car?"

"What car?"

"In the parking lot."

"No."

"You and Ted were in the back seat."

"No."

"And then you got sick."

"I did?"

"Come on, Jane. You must remember."

"No," she says, shaking her head. "I don't."

A thought pops into my mind. Jane thinks she has no experience with boys. But the truth is, she has plenty of experience. She just doesn't remember.

"You shouldn't drink," I tell her.

"I drank too much . . . that's all."

"You shouldn't drink at all if you can't handle it."

"It makes me feel good. It loosens me up. Otherwise I'm shy around boys."

"You'd never know it from last night."

"That's exactly what I'm trying to tell you!" Jane gets out of bed. "I've got to take a shower. Will you come to church with us?"

"I don't think so," I say.

"Please, Davey. I can't stand the idea of being alone with my parents this morning."

I don't respond.

"As a friend," Jane says. "Do it as a friend."

"Oh, all right," I say.

"Thanks, I won't forget this."

Jane dashes down the hall to the bathroom and I begin to get dressed wondering why I am feeling so angry at her. Was it the drinking? No, I don't think so. Then what? The making out in the back seat? Yes, maybe. But why? Because I wanted to be making out too? Because I wanted to feel strong arms around me again? Is that it?

There are more churches in Los Alamos than I have ever seen anywhere. There is a church on practically every corner. I don't know if it's because scientists pray more than other people, or what. Maybe they have more guilt and fear. I once read an article in *Time* magazine that said organized religion is based on guilt and fear. I wouldn't know. Both of my parents are half Jewish. For a while we went to the Unitarian Fellowship in Atlantic City, and after that we tried Temple Sinai. Now we don't go anywhere.

That afternoon I go to the canyon, hoping to find Wolf. It is cold and gray. I wait for two hours, but he doesn't show. I ride home slowly with tears in my eyes. I can't seem to get rid of the empty feeling that started last night and won't go away.

TWENTY-THREE

"Do you think we'll go home for Christmas?" I ask Mom. She is in bed, reading. She puts her book aside and makes room for me to sit on the bed, next to her. I stretch out, examine my fingernails and begin to peel off the putrid purple polish.

"I thought you understood," Mom says.

"Understood what?"

"That we're staying for the school year."

"No," I say, sitting straight up. "You never said that. Nobody ever said that."

"I can't go back, Davey."

"What are you talking about . . . what do you mean, you can't go back?" I drop the bits of polish that I have peeled off my nails. They scatter to the floor like tiny flowers that have died.

"I can't go back now," Mom says. "I'm not ready. There's still too much to deal with. I'm just beginning to get myself together. I have a long way to go."

"Why didn't you tell me?" I ask. "All this time I've been thinking that we'll be home by Christmas."

"No, honey. That would be the worst time to

go home. Don't you see? Besides, you're all set in school now. It wouldn't make sense to pull you out in the middle of the year. And Jason is happy too. This is a nice place. You like it, don't you?"

"I don't know. Some days I do and some days I don't. But I never thought we were staying. Never."

"Well, neither did I," Mom says, "but Bitsy and Walter are such a help and they want us to stay."

"Do I have to keep eating bran in my cereal?"

Mom laughs.

"Do I?"

"It's good for you."

I bend over and pick the tiny ovals of polish from the floor, cupping them in my hand.

"If we are staying then I want to learn to ski. Everyone is talking about ski season. If there's enough snow the ski area will be open before Christmas."

"We'll talk about it with Walter and Bitsy," Mom says. "Okay?"

When we do, Walter says, "It's out of the question."

"But everyone skis," I tell him.

"That's an exaggeration," Walter says.

"Well, maybe not everybody, because you and Bitsy don't . . . but Jane's whole family skis, except for her mother."

"I'm not going to argue about this, Davey," Walter says. "My mind is made up. I'll give you my reasons. Number one, it's dangerous. Number two, it's expensive. Number three, it's an overrated, trendy sport. You can go ice skating instead. We have a very nice skating pond that will be frozen soon."

"But I already know how to ice skate," I tell him.

"Good. Then you're all set."

"You don't understand," I say.

"That's what you say to us every time we don't respond in the way you want us to respond."

I feel frustrated, unsure of what Walter has just said. Walter twists words and confuses me. It's impossible to argue with him and win. So I shout, "Dammit . . ."

And Walter says, calmly, "Let's keep emotion out of this conversation. Let's hold it to logic, pure and simple."

I look over to my mother for support. "I'm sure Walter knows much more about skiing than we do, Davey," she says.

"But he doesn't ski," I argue.

"Maybe not," Mom says, "but he knows *about* it."

"Besides," Bitsy says, "we know a family whose daughter was on the ski team and she crashed into a tree, head first, and wound up a vegetable in an Albuquerque hospital. They visit her every Sunday but she doesn't recognize them. You don't want to wind up a vegetable, do you?"

"What kind of vegetable?" Jason asks.

"She's probably better off than I am!" I shout. "She doesn't have to live in this house."

"What's wrong with this house?" Bitsy says.

"What *kind* of vegetable?" Jason asks again.

"A turnip!" I tell him, storming out of the room.

"Really," Jason says. "A turnip?"

TWENTY-FOUR

I look forward to candy striping each week, especially to my visit with Mr. Ortiz. He is the only patient who has been in the hospital since my first day there. We have become friends. But it's hard for me to see him losing his strength. Each week there is a change for the worse. His cheeks are sunken now and his body seems to be withering away. Last week I saw him without his dental bridge and he looked ancient, even though I know from his chart that he is only fifty-seven. Through it all he remains cheerful. I don't understand how someone so sick, so close to death can still enjoy what little of life is left.

Mr. Ortiz likes to hear about school and he has decided that I should go out for the swim team. I have explained a dozen times that I can't dive, that I hardly ever swim with my face in the water but he says I can learn, that I am built like a swimmer. He regrets never having learned to swim himself but his son was the star of the high school team and for three years Mr. Ortiz never missed a meet. I promise him that I will think about swimming but the truth is, I am more interested in trying out for the school play. It's going to be a production of *Oklahoma!* and scripts and music are available at the drama department office, even though tryouts are still a few months away. I doubt that a sophomore has a chance at a major role but there is always the chorus and it would be nice to sing again, outside of the shower.

When I am candy striping I save Mr. Ortiz' room for last, so that I can spend extra time with him. Today, as I walk down the corridor, I see that his door is closed and I get a sinking feeling. I have told myself over and over that I must prepare for Mr. Ortiz' death. But I haven't been able to. Not yet.

I knock softly on the door, then push it open and feel a great sense of relief when I see Mr. Ortiz lying in his bed. "Come," he says softly, when he sees that it is me. "Come and meet my son."

I look across the room. His son stands with his back to me. His hands are pressed against the window frame.

"Martin," Mr. Ortiz says, "this is Davey."

Martin turns around and I can't believe it! It is Wolf.

We stare at each other. Finally he says, "Hello," as if we have never met.

I try to say hello too, but my voice cracks. I cough, clear my throat twice, and say it again. "Hello."

"Martin was captain of the swim team," Mr.

Ortiz says, "and co-captain of the soccer team, and a National Merit Scholarship winner and runner-up in the Westinghouse Science Contest and . . ."

"Come on, Dad," Wolf says gently. He looks at the floor and refuses to meet my eyes. His hair tumbles across his face.

"He doesn't like to talk about himself," Mr. Ortiz says.

As if I don't already know.

"And now he's got a full scholarship to Cal Tech," Mr. Ortiz continues. "He's a junior and he's going to be a brilliant physicist . . ."

"Hey, Dad . . ." Wolf says, "give me a break." Wolf finally looks directly at me as if to say, *Don't listen to any of this crap. That's not the real me.* He is embarrassed by his father's enthusiastic outburst but doesn't want to hurt his feelings either. I want to tell him that it's okay. That I understand.

"You should be proud," Mr. Ortiz tells him. "Look at all you've done in your life and you're only twenty years old." Mr. Ortiz closes his eyes. Talking this much has worn him down. When he opens them again his voice is weaker and I have to stand close to hear what he is saying. "So what do you think . . . I'm a lucky man, no?"

"Yes," I say.

"And he's handsome too."

I nod.

"Some day he's going to have a big job at the

Lab. Group leader . . . division leader . . . maybe even Director."

"We'll see, Dad," Wolf says. "We'll see."

Mr. Ortiz holds the dancing bear out to Wolf. "Wind it for her," he says. "She likes to see it dance."

Wolf winds up the bear and sets it on the table, where it dances in circles, until it wears down, moving more and more slowly until it stops completely. Like Mr. Ortiz, I think.

Mr. Ortiz closes his eyes and whispers, "I have to sleep now."

Wolf kisses his father's cheek. "See you tonight, Dad."

We walk out of the room together. At first we don't speak. We walk down the corridor to the elevator and I push the button.

"You're surprised to see me here," Wolf says.

Surprised is an understatement. "Yes," I tell him. "I'm surprised. Aren't you surprised to see me?"

"Sure."

"How come I haven't seen you here before?" I ask.

"I've been working at the Lab in the afternoons. I took the semester off to be with my father. I usually visit here at night."

The elevator door opens and we step into it. There are two nurses and a doctor standing to one side.

"I'll drive you home," Wolf says.

"I have to get my things," I tell him.

"I'll wait outside," he says.

"Okay . . . I'll only be a minute."

I grab my jacket and books from the closet in the volunteers' office and dash down the hall to the revolving door. Jane is there, waiting for me, her hat pulled down over her forehead.

"I've got a ride home," I tell her. I push my way through the revolving door. Jane is right behind me. Outside, Wolf waits in a battered Toyota pick-up truck. He toots his horn at me. I wave. "See you tomorrow," I tell Jane. She looks confused and hurt. I don't blame her but I don't have the time to explain now.

I get into Wolf's truck and we take off. "I live in the western area," I say, "only a few blocks from here . . . on 45th Street."

Wolf nods. He knows his way around town.

"I didn't know you were going to be a physicist," I say, glancing sideways at him.

"I don't know if I am," Wolf says.

"But your father said . . ."

"It's what he wants for me."

"You must be very smart," I say.

Wolf laughs.

I fiddle with the pom pom on my hat, which I hold on my lap. "What did you mean, it's what *he* wants?"

"Just that. He has my life all planned."

I think about Mr. Ortiz and the way he decided I should go out for the swim team, without finding out if I have an interest in swimming. I think about Jane's parents and how her father wants her to go to MIT and her mother wants her to go to Wellesley. I think about Walter and the way he is pushing me to go to college without finding out what's important to me. I nod at Wolf. I understand what he is saying. "What do *you* want?" I ask him.

"That's the big question, Tiger," he says. "And I haven't come up with the answer yet."

"This is it," I say, as we pull up in front of the house.

Wolf turns off the engine and looks at me. "Did your father die of cancer? Is that why you're so close to mine?"

"No," I say. "My father . . ." I pause, about to tell him the truth. But then I change my mind and say, "My father died suddenly."

"It's tough either way," he says, "isn't it?"

"Yes."

He rests his head on his arms on the steering wheel. I lean over and touch his hand. "Will I see you at the canyon over the weekend?"

"No, I'm spending all of my time with my father now."

I nod. "Then I'll see you next week, at the hospital."

He doesn't respond and even as I say it I know that by next week it could be over. That by then Mr. Ortiz could be dead. I open the door on my side of the truck.

Wolf sits up. "Goodbye, Tiger."

I nod again. If I try to speak now I know I will cry. I get out of the truck and run into the house.

"Who was that in the pick-up truck?" Jane asks the next day.

"A friend."

"I know that. But who?"

"Mr. Ortiz' son."

"He's cute."

"There are things that matter more than being cute!" I snap.

Jane's face turns red and tears spring to her eyes.

I walk away feeling like a creep.

That night I call her. "I'm sorry."

"I don't know what's wrong with you, Davey," Jane says.

"Nothing," I tell her. "It's just hard to see Mr. Ortiz dying . . . that's all."

"We're not supposed to become emotionally involved with the patients."

"I know . . . but I'm human . . . I can't help it."

There is a long pause. Finally Jane says, "Look, we're going down to Santa Fe on Saturday to do some last minute Christmas shopping. You want to come?"

"Sure," I say. "I'd like that."

* * *

At dinner the next night my mother says, "I'm thinking seriously of looking for a job after Christmas. Something part time."

"A Casual," Walter suggests, buttering his baked potato.

"A casual what?" I ask.

"That's what we call part time employees at the Lab," Walter explains. "I think I can help," he tells Mom. "Maybe pull a few strings."

"That would be wonderful," Mom says. "I've got to get into a routine. I need some place to go every morning. A reason to get out of bed."

"I get out of bed because I have to pee," Jason says.

"Not at the table," Bitsy tells him.

"No, not at the table," Jason says. "In the bathroom."

I begin to laugh. Once I get started I can't stop. I laugh and I laugh, until my side is splitting.

TWENTY-FIVE

In Santa Fe I feel so exhilarated, I can't get enough of the street life and the people. I realize that one of the things I miss most about Atlantic City is people-watching. I used to go to the Boardwalk and just watch, fascinated. In Los Alamos there is no one to watch, except the housewives in the supermarket and even they have a sameness I find boring. In Santa Fe, the tourists mingle with the natives—the Spanish, the Anglos, the Native Americans, all together.

We walk around the Plaza, admiring the windows of the shops and the festive decorations. This part of Santa Fe seems to be a village, not a city. It reminds me of *Christmas in Other Lands,* a book we studied in fourth grade. I feel as if I am in another land. I see a window full of piñatas. I want to buy one for our family, but when I go into the store and price them they are too expensive.

The Palace of the Governors dates back to 1609, Jane tells me. Groups of Indians sit under its portal, displaying their wares on colorful blankets. There are delicate silver and turquoise earrings and necklaces, strings of heishi, chunky silver bracelets and rings. I want to buy something for my mother. I go from blanket to blanket admiring everything and finally decide on a pair of earrings. They are ten dollars, which is more than I can afford but I splurge because they are so pretty.

After a while we go to the French Pastry Shop which is adjacent to La Fonda Hotel. We order apricot tarts and herb tea. When we have finished Jane asks her parents if she and I can shop on our own for the rest of the afternoon.

"Yes, but be careful," her mother says. "Stay off the side streets and don't speak to any strangers."

Outside, the Albertsons head in one direction, and Jane and I in the other. As we are walking up Palace Avenue, a group of boys comes toward us. Jane clutches my arm.

"What is it?" I ask. She is trembling.

"They're Spanish," she whispers.

"So?"

"Don't look at them. Look away. Look across the street."

"Jane . . ." I say and start to laugh.

"Do you know how high the rape statistics are in this town?" she whispers.

"No," I tell her.

"High."

"Nobody's going to rape you in the middle of the afternoon, in the middle of town."

"Don't be so sure."

The boys pass us.

"You see," Jane says. "Didn't I tell you?"

"What?"

"Didn't you hear them?"

"Hear them what?"

"Make those sounds."

"No," I say. "I didn't hear anything. I don't think they even noticed us."

"They're all like that," Jane says anyway. "They're all out to rape Anglo girls."

"Jane, that is one of the craziest things I've ever heard!" We stop walking and face each other.

"You're new around here," she says. "You don't understand."

I think of Wolf and inside my head I say *No, you're the one who doesn't understand.*

We browse in the Villagra Bookstore, where I find a paperback copy of *Computing for Fun.* I think of Walter immediately. He could use a little fun, and since he is so into computers, I buy it for him.

I get a small leather pouch for Jason, in a shop down the street. He can keep marbles in it, or stones he has found, or shells, when we go back home. I know he will like it.

At Doodlets, a funny little shop crammed full of gifts with cat motifs, I get Bitsy a pot holder with a cat face on it and a set of catnip toys for Minka. I buy two rolls of cat wrapping paper, and while Jane is off searching for gifts for her family, I bought her a cat mobile, to hang in her room. There, my shopping is finished. I feel very good about it. I am almost wiped out financially, but maybe I can pick up a babysitting job over the holidays. And then I see the candle. It is round, with five wicks on top, and depicts the New Mexican sunset. My father would love it, I think. He collected unusual candles and then waited for special occasions to light them.

"Would you like one?" a saleswoman says to me. "They're just $3.95."

"Yes," I tell her, "but I'm going to have to return one of these rolls of wrapping paper."

"All right," she says. "I'll credit you $2.50 for the paper." I reach into my wallet and pull out my last two dollars. The saleswoman wraps the candle in tissue paper and I put it into the bag with the other gifts.

I won't tell anyone I bought a present for my father. Who would understand?

Jane and I meet her parents for an early dinner at The Steaksmith, and when we come out of the restaurant the farolitos, which line the flat topped roofs of the buildings downtown, have been lit. They are candles set in sand, inside brown paper bags, and are the traditional New Mexican Christmas decorations. The Plaza looks beautiful, outlined in soft lights.

Jane's parents walk hand in hand. Tonight, they remind me of my parents, happy and loving. Tears come to my eyes. This must be a very hard time of year for my mother, I think. Facing the holidays without Daddy.

When we get back to the car we see that someone has written on the hood with a magic marker. *Los Alamos Sucks!*

The Albertsons don't say anything. But they look at each other in a way that lets me know this isn't the first time it has happened.

"How did they know we were from Los Alamos?" I ask Jane.

"The LASL sticker," she says.

"Oh, right. I forgot." Every car that has parking privileges at the Lab has an ID sticker in the front window.

It makes me angry, this two-way hatred. I don't understand it. I wonder how much of it is caused by fear?

The lovely mood is spoiled. I fall asleep on the ride home.

TWENTY-SIX

On Christmas morning Bitsy brings out a menorah. "It belonged to *your* great-grandmother," she tells Jason and me. Even though Hanukkah fell early this year we light all eight candles and recite the Hanukkah blessing. Then we go into the living room and open our presents, which are under the tree. It is nice to celebrate both holidays, I think. If I ever have kids that's what I'll do.

We have a quiet Christmas, a sad Christmas, although each of us pretends to be happy, pretends to be excited by our gifts. Underneath we are all thinking the same thing. It is our first Christmas without Daddy. But we don't talk about it.

Bitsy and Walter have invited some people in for Christmas dinner. Two men from the Lab, both of them divorced and lonely, a single woman they have known for years and a young kindergarten teacher who belongs to Bitsy's Tuesday night group. I think it is nice that Bitsy and Walter have asked these people to join us, even though the kindergarten teacher drinks too much wine and gets silly, and I don't like the way one of the divorced men keeps looking at my mother.

That night, when the company has left, when the dishes have been washed and dried and put away, I go to my room and take my father's present out of the trunk. "Daddy . . . this is for you." I light all five wicks on the candle and watch as the New Mexican sunset disappears. "Merry Christmas, Daddy. I wish you were here." In fifteen minutes there is nothing left. Nothing at all, except a pile of wax.

The next day it snows. I sit in front of the picture window in the living room, watching the flakes fall. My breath makes the glass frosty.

TWENTY-SEVEN

Mr. Ortiz is in a coma. He will probably never wake up. Wolf sits at his bedside, an opened book on his lap. But he's not reading. He never turns the pages. I ask if I can get anything for him.

"A Coke would be good," he says.

I bring him one, from the machine.

The nurses on the floor assure me that Mr. Ortiz is not in pain. That soon it will be over.

That evening, Wolf drives me home. "I'm going to miss you, Tiger," he says.

"What do you mean?" I ask. "Where are you going?"

"Away."

"Now?"

"No, but soon. After . . ."

"Will I see you again?"

"Yes."

"When?"

He thinks for a minute. Then he says, *"Cuando los lagartijos corren."*

"What does that mean?"

"Look it up," he says, and he smiles. It is the first time I have seen him smile in a long time.

"I'm going to miss you too," I tell him.

He takes me in his arms and we don't speak again. He holds me close, patting my hair. I rest my cheek against the rough wool of his sweater.

"Who was that?" Bitsy asks, when I go inside.

"Who was who?"

"In that truck . . . outside . . . just now . . ."

"Oh, that was a friend of mine," I say, anxious to get up to my room. I want to write down what Wolf has just said to me, before I forget it.

"What friend?" Bitsy asks.

"You don't know him."

"Maybe I do."

"His name is Martin Ortiz," I say, walking toward the stairs.

"Ortiz?" Bitsy repeats, following me.

"Yes."

"Does he go to the high school?"

"Not anymore."

"He's a dropout?"

"I didn't say that."

"Well, why don't you just tell me about him, Davey . . . instead of playing Twenty Questions."

"You're the one playing Twenty Questions, not me," I say.

Bitsy takes a deep breath. "Is he Spanish?"

"I guess."

"You *guess?*"

"I never asked him."

"Where is he from, Española?"

"No, he's from here. He's from Los Alamos."

"He is?"

"Yes. He works at the Lab."

"What does he do there . . . maintenance?"

I almost laugh. I almost laugh and say, *Yes, he picks up the garbage,* just to see her reaction. But I don't. I am very polite. I say, "His father is a patient at the Medical Center. He goes to Cal Tech but he's taking the semester off."

"Well," Bitsy says, her voice full of relief. "Why didn't you say so in the first place?"

I hold up my hands as if to say *search me,* then race up the stairs to my room. I take out my notebook and write *Quando los lagartihose koren.* I know I haven't spelled it correctly, but at least I will remember it this way. Tomorrow I will go to the Spanish department at school and ask one of the teachers what it means.

"*Cuando los lagartijos corren,*" Mr. Valdez says, writing it down in my notebook.

"Oh," I say, embarrassed by my errors. "What does it mean?"

"It means, *when the lizards run.* Does that make sense to you?" he asks.

I smile. "Yes," I tell him. "Yes, it does." I try saying it myself. *"Cuando los lagartijos corren."*

"You've got a good ear," Mr. Valdez says. "You should take Spanish."

"I'm going to . . . next year," I say.

Cuando los lagartijos corren . . . when the lizards run, I say to myself all during my next class, which is Geometry. *I'll see Wolf in the springtime, in the canyon.* I say it over and over inside my head, until the teacher calls on me to draw a trapezoidal figure on the board and I have no idea what she's talking about.

My mother has been hired as a Casual at the Lab. She moves around from group to group, depending on who needs her services, like a substitute teacher. She types and files and answers the phone. And she likes it. It makes her feel useful again, she says. It gives her a sense of purpose. I am not about to argue with her but I can't see typing at the Lab as useful or having much to do with purpose. It seems to me she would have more purpose by being a real mother to Jason and me.

On Saturday morning, during breakfast, I decide to bring up the subject of Driver's Ed. I've been thinking about it ever since Reuben mentioned it in the car the night Jane got drunk. The notice just went up on the bulletin board outside the office at school. You have to sign up before February first to get into the spring class. I hand out information to my mother, and to Bitsy and Walter, asking them to read it when they have a chance. Then I go upstairs to clean my room. I want to drive so badly. If only I could drive I could get to Santa Fe. I could watch the people and browse around and most of all just get out of this town. This town suffers from a chronic case of the blahs.

An hour later I am folding the laundry with my mother, while Jason and Bitsy bake an angel food cake. Walter sits at the table, a mess of papers spread out in front of him. He is working on his mini-computer.

"So if I sign up now I've got a good chance of being accepted into Driver's Ed this spring." I say it quietly. If I keep emotion out of my voice I will do better with Walter and I know that he is the one I've got to convince.

"Fifteen is much too young for Driver's Ed," Walter says, not even looking up from his computer.

"I'll be sixteen in April."

"There's just no reason to rush it, Davey," Bitsy says. She cracks several eggs, separating the whites from the yolks.

"Everyone my age is signing up," I say, as I fold a towel in thirds. "Jane's parents gave her permission." I am quiet and matter of fact, as if I don't really care at all.

"When you're a senior . . . that's time enough," Walter says, over his shoulder.

"But that's two years from now. How am I supposed to get around until then?"

"You can walk," Walter says. "Or you can ride a bicycle. You've managed until now. You'll manage a little longer."

I face Mom and say, "Mom, please. I really want to take Driver's Ed. It's very important to me. All you have to do is sign the little green card."

Mom looks at me and we make eye contact for the first time in months. Then, just as she is about to speak, Walter says, "Statistics show that accidents, especially automobile accidents, are the leading cause of death among young people."

"Why go looking for trouble?" Bitsy says. She pours the batter into the cake pan and Jason pulls the oven door open for her.

"Mom . . . say something . . . will you?"

"Walter and Bitsy know what's best," Mom says.

"Since when . . . since when I'd like to know?" I explode now. I don't care about logic or emotion or anything. "Can't you think for yourself anymore? Do you have to let them decide everything?" I spin around. Jason is drinking a glass of milk and listening intently. I turn back to my mother and point my finger at her, accusingly. "You're getting to be just like them . . . you know that . . . just like them!"

"That's enough!" Walter shouts, slamming his hand on the table.

"No, it's not enough!" I shout back. "I'm sick of hearing how dangerous everything is."

"Driving a car *is* dangerous," Mom says.

"Oh, please . . . spare me, will you?" I yell

at Mom. "Dangerous . . . dangerous . . . dangerous . . . *Stay out of the canyon, Davey . . . you could be hit by a falling rock. Don't forget your bicycle helmet, Davey . . . you could get hit by a car. No, you can't learn to ski, Davey . . . you might wind up a vegetable!*"I am really yelling now.

"Davey, honey . . ." Mom begins and she reaches for me. But I pull away from her.

"Some people have lived up here so long they've forgotten what the real world is like," I shout, "and the idea of it scares the . . ."

"You can just stop it, right now," Walter says, before I have finished. He says it slowly, making every word count.

"You're a good one to talk," I tell him. "You're the one who's making the bombs. You're the one who's figuring out how to blow up the whole world. But you won't let me take Driver's Ed. A person can get killed crossing the street. A person can get killed minding his own store. Did you ever think of that?" I kick the wall and stomp out of the room. I am crying hard and my throat feels sore.

"We have a long way to go with that girl," I hear Walter mutter.

Then Mom says, "It's hard to be fifteen."

TWENTY-EIGHT

Walter's Chamber Music group is giving a concert at our house. Bitsy tells me to wear a skirt.

"What for?" I say.

"It's a dress up concert," she answers. "It's a festive occasion."

"It's not *my* concert," I tell her. "It's not a festive occasion to *me.*"

Bitsy taps her foot and glares at me.

"Oh, all right," I say. "If it's that important to you I'll wear a skirt."

I run upstairs, feeling angry. Partly at Bitsy and partly at myself. I don't mean to act rude but sometimes I can't help myself. Bitsy and Walter say that ever since the Driver's Ed incident I have a chip on my shoulder. They say that as long as I live in their house I have to live by their rules. Maybe so. But that doesn't mean I have to like them, or even accept them. I toss on the skirt Mom gave me for Christmas. It is blue denim and tiered and the truth is, I like it. I don't mind changing out of my jeans. I might have done it on my own. It was having Bitsy *tell* me to do it that got my back up. I wear the skirt with boots and a loose white sweater. I have to pick a dozen cat hairs off it. Minka must have been sleeping in my sweater drawer. When I forget to close my dresser drawers she hops right in and makes herself at home.

I am the only one in the living room when the doorbell rings. I open the door. It is Ned Grodzinski, one of the men who came to our house for Christmas dinner. He is filling in tonight for the woman who usually plays violin.

"Hello, Darby," Ned says, stuttering over the D.

"It's Davey," I tell him. Ned looks like the nerd in the National Lampoon poster. He carries six pens in his shirt pocket, his high-water pants show off his white socks and his hair is short and slicked down. He is also the one who kept staring at my mother on Christmas Day. I am not overjoyed to see him again.

Fortunately I don't have to spend any time alone with him. The doorbell rings every few minutes and soon the house is filled with guests. Jason and I sit on the floor in front of the fireplace. The others sit on the sofas and a group of chairs from the dining room which Bitsy has arranged in rows. The musicians tune up and the concert begins.

Walter plays the viola, a woman with a long, gray braid plays the violin, a bald man with a beard is on cello and Ned plays second violin.

Jason yawns constantly. Every time I see him yawn, I yawn, although it is only eight o'clock and neither one of us should feel tired. There is something about chamber music that makes you want to go to sleep. Maybe that's why they call it chamber music.

When the concert is finally over everyone applauds and Bitsy serves coffee and cake. Jason and I both stuff ourselves.

Bitsy pours a cup for The Nerd and says, "Ned, you remember our sister-in-law, Gwen Wexler, don't you?"

"How could I forget?" Ned says, and this time he doesn't stutter at all.

Mom shakes his hand and says, "The concert was just lovely."

"My regular group plays on Fridays," Ned tells Mom.

Bitsy is all smiles as she excuses herself and moves on to her other guests.

I stay close to Mom.

"Would you like to hear us sometime?" Ned asks her.

"When?" Mom says.

"This Friday . . . next . . . the week after . . ."

"Well," Mom says, laughing, only it's not her regular laugh. It's a high pitched, nervous kind of laugh.

"I'm divorced," Ned says.

"Yes, I know," Mom says. "I'm a widow."

I can't believe this.

"Walter told me," Ned says, nodding seriously.

Jason whispers something to me but I shake him away. I am steaming. Why doesn't Mom just tell The Nerd to bug off? Why is she going through this *I'm a widow* business?

"So," Ned says, "I hear you're working at the Lab now."

"Well, I'm only a Casual," Mom says. "What group are *you* in?"

She is beginning to sound just like one of them.

"I'm in H Division. H is for Health."

H is for *hick*, I think. H is for *horrible*. H is for *hyena*.

Now Mom and The Nerd stand silently and just look at each other. I can't understand why she would waste her time talking to him.

"Will you have lunch with me tomorrow?" Ned finally says.

"Tomorrow?" Mom repeats.

She is acting so dumb I want to slug her.

"Yes, tomorrow," he says. "And if you say *no* I won't bother you again. I don't know how to go about this anyway. I'm beginning to feel very foolish."

Good, I think. Now, just say *no*, Mom, and that will be the end of it.

But instead, Mom says, "Yes, I'll have lunch with you."

"Great!" Ned is so pleased he can't stop grinning. "Do you know where you'll be working tomorrow?"

"P division."

"I'll pick you up outside at noon. I have a white Datsun but it's dirty so it looks gray."

Mom laughs. "I'm sure we'll recognize each other."

"Well, then . . . see you tomorrow."

"Right."

Later, when everyone has gone home, I go up to Mom's room. She is looking in the mirror, holding a red sweater up to her face. "What do you think?" she asks me.

"I can't understand why you said you'd have lunch with him," I tell her. "He's such a nerd!"

"Oh, come on, honey . . . he's a nice man. He's shy, that's all."

"I can't believe you're going out on a date."

"It's not a date," Mom says, putting the red sweater away. "We're having lunch together, that's all."

"I call that a date," I say.

"Well, I don't," Mom answers.

TWENTY-NINE

On Tuesday afternoon, when I get to the Medical Center, I save a rose from one of the floral arrangements I've delivered to a patient and carry it down the hall, to Mr. Ortiz' room. But when I get there the room is empty. The bed has been stripped. I race down the hall to the nurses' station. "Mr. Ortiz?" I say.

The nurse shakes her head. "Last night," she says.

"No!"

"I'm sorry, Davey. We all felt the same way about him."

I choke up and clutch the stem of the rose so hard a thorn goes through my skin. I cry out, half from the pain in my finger and half from the pain of losing Mr. Ortiz.

"His son asked me to give you these," the nurse says, opening a drawer. She pulls out the dancing bear and an envelope and hands them both to me. I open the envelope.

Tiger,

He wanted you to have the bear. Remem-

ber him as he was—full of life—full of love. I'll see you cuando los lagartijos corren.

Wolf

I put the note back in its envelope and hold the dancing bear to my face. I can't stop crying. I am crying harder now than when my father died. Then, I was just numb. Now I feel everything.

I go downstairs, to the volunteers' office and explain to the director that I have to go home. I tell her I have a headache, which is true. My head is pounding. The director tells me to go home and take two aspirin. She thinks I am probably coming down with the flu.

I run all the way home, sweating inside my down jacket.

When I get there Jason is in the kitchen, wearing an apron.

"What are you doing?" I shout.

"What does it look like I'm doing?"

"And why are you wearing that faggy apron?"

"So I don't get messed up," he says.

"Where's Mom?"

"She's not home yet."

"Where's Bitsy?"

"She went to Safeway. Ned's coming to dinner."

"That nerd!"

"He's nice," Jason says, and he keeps on cutting out gingerbread man cookies.

"God, Jason . . . just look at you!" I yell. "Is

this how you're going to spend the rest of your life?"

"What do you mean?"

"Like this . . . baking cookies? I can't stand what's happening to you! I can't stand what's happening to us!"

"What are you talking about? I like baking cookies."

"That's *not* what I'm talking about!" I go upstairs, throw myself down on my bed, and wind up the dancing bear. I hang over the side of the bed and watch him turning circles on the floor. Why did I have to take it out on Jason? I ask myself. He's just a little kid. What does he know? Besides, what happened to my fantasy of Jason Wexler, Cookie Specialist? Just thinking about that sets me off crying again.

"I want to go home," I say aloud. "I want to go home to Atlantic City."

Later, I decide to write a letter.

Dear Wolf,

I'm really sorry about your father. I liked him a lot, as you know. Thanks for remembering about the bear. I'm going to keep him on my bedside table. He will remind me of your father and of you, not that I need reminding, but you know what I mean.

I told you that my father died suddenly. Well, that's true, but it's not like you think.

He was shot in the chest during a robbery last summer. I couldn't tell you the truth before. I couldn't tell anyone. Here's the thing, Wolf—your father was ready to die. Mine wasn't. You were prepared for your father's death. I wasn't. After it happened I was afraid. I was so afraid! Of everything. Of going to school. Of just going to sleep at night. I was afraid of you, that first day in the canyon. I was planning to bash in your head with a rock, if you made a false move. Lucky for you, you didn't.

I don't want to go through life afraid. But I don't want to wind up like my father, either. Sometimes I think about dying and it scares me, because it's so permanent. I mean, once it's over, it's over. Unless there is something that comes after. Something that we don't know about. I like the idea of an afterlife but I can't bring myself to really believe in it. Do you?

Here is something I found in a magazine:

> *Each of us must confront our own fears, must come face to face with them. How we handle our fears will determine where we go with the rest of our lives. To experience adventure or to be limited by the fear of it.*

I think about that a lot, especially in this town, where so many people seem afraid.

Does building bombs make them feel afraid, or is it the isolation from the rest of the world? Have you figured it out? If you have, please let me know.

I have to go now. I will remember your father as you asked me to, full of life and full of love. I will see you cuando los lagartijos corren . . .

Love,
Tiger

I take the letter to school the next day and look up the address for Cal Tech in the guidance office. I mail it at lunchtime.

THIRTY

My letter to Wolf is returned on the same day that my first semester grades come in. The envelope is stamped *Moved—No Forwarding Address.* Where is he? I wonder. What is he doing? I put the letter into the trunk next to ones I have received from Lenaya, who writes to me on the first day of every month. In the spring, I will personally hand my letter to Wolf. In the spring, when I see him again.

I show my grades to my mother, who is getting ready to go out to dinner with The Nerd. She says, "Very nice, Davey . . . especially since you missed more than a month of school. I'm sure you did your best."

"How come you're going out on another date with *him*?" I ask.

"It's not a date," Mom says. "We're having dinner together, that's all."

"Sure," I say.

Mom turns away from the mirror, where she has been brushing her hair. "I need the adult companionship."

"I thought you had that all day at the Lab."

"No, this is different," she tells me.

"Well, have a good time," I say, but I don't mean it and Mom knows that I don't. Then I go downstairs to feed Minka.

Later, Walter asks to see my grades, and when I show them to him he hits the roof.

"They're not *that* bad," I say. I got a C in American Cultures, a C in Geometry, a B– in French, a B in English and an A in Typing. "Mom thought they were fine, especially since I missed the first six weeks of school."

"With a little effort you could have had all A's and B's," Walter says. "You don't apply yourself. You don't work up to your full potential."

"How do you know?" I ask. "I do plenty of studying in school and plenty in my room, at night." This is not exactly true. I almost never study at school, except for geometry. I do my geometry homework with Reuben, because he's very good at math. I used to be, but I guess missing all that school really did matter. And at night, I do only what is absolutely necessary. "Besides," I say, "what difference does it make? It's what you learn that counts, not what grades you get."

"Who told you that?" Walter asks.

"My father."

"I should have guessed."

"What's *that* supposed to mean?"

"You want to wind up like *him?*" Walter says, raising his voice. "With no education . . .

working in a 7-Eleven store . . . a wasted life . . ."

"How dare you say that my father had a wasted life! You don't know anything." My stomach is all tied up in knots. I am on the verge of tears. "And I'm going to tell Mom what you said about my father. He was a better man than you. In every way."

"Fine!" Walter booms. "You tell your mother. Or maybe I'll save you the trouble and tell her for you. Because if your father had been a *better* man she wouldn't be where she is now."

"That's not true!" I shout.

"Your mother is another example of a wasted life."

"What?" I say. "What did you say about my mother?"

"Pregnant in high school and destitute at thirty-four."

"Shut up . . . just shut up . . ." I rush toward him, calling him every name in the book, and pound on his chest with my fists.

He grabs me by the wrist and smacks me. Hard. Right across the face.

"I hate you," I yell. "I've always hated you." I turn and run out of the room and as I do I see that Bitsy and Jason have been in the kitchen the whole time, listening.

Upstairs, I get into bed and when I have calmed down enough, I write another letter to Wolf. Even though I have no address for him and can't mail it, I have to tell someone what is happening. I have to tell someone how my life is falling apart. Someone who will understand.

An hour later Walter knocks on my bedroom door. "Davey, can I come in for a minute?"

"I have nothing to say to you," I tell him.

"But I have something to say to you."

"Suit yourself."

He opens the door. "I'm sorry," he says. "I certainly didn't mean to insult your parents."

I don't take my eyes off the dancing bear, which I am holding in my lap.

"I just hoped you'd realize how important education is."

I still don't look at him but I say, "I might want to be a professional singer."

"I had no idea," he says. "I've never heard you sing. Are you any good?"

I don't answer.

He lowers his voice. "I'm sorry I slapped you. That was uncalled for and unplanned. I don't believe in violence."

Very funny, I think. All those bombs and missiles but he doesn't believe in violence.

"Can you forgive me?" he asks.

Without speaking I put the dancing bear on my night table, snap off the lamp, roll over in bed and close my eyes.

After a minute Walter leaves. I hear him walking down the hall.

THIRTY-ONE

Jane has promised to try out for *Oklahoma!* with me. We are to meet outside the auditorium, after school. I get there first, and watch groups of kids file inside. So many people are trying out. Do I even have a chance? I begin to feel anxious and after ten minutes, when Jane still hasn't shown, I think about chickening out and going home.

But then Jane comes staggering down the hall. "Hi . . ." she says, all bright-eyed. "Here I am. Ready and willing."

I smell the booze on her breath. "Have you been drinking?" I say. Of course she has. Why do I bother to ask.

"Just a teensy-weensy bit," Jane says, giggling.

It is not the first time that Jane has gotten drunk in school. But I can't believe she would do this today. "You can't try out drunk," I tell her.

"Then I can't try out . . . because I'm not getting up there sober . . . that's for sure."

I look at her a minute, shake my head, then say, "Come on . . . let's go." We walk into the auditorium and find two seats together.

Mr. Vanderhoot is directing the play, with Ms.

Dersh, the head of the music department. She announces that she will call three names from the beginning of the alphabet, then three names from the end, until everyone who has signed up has had a turn.

We go through Abel and Ackerman before Ms. Dersh says, "Jane Albertson."

"Here I am," Jane calls.

"Tell them you've changed your mind," I whisper, grabbing hold of her sleeve.

"No," she says, shaking me off. She walks up the aisle to the steps, leading to the stage. I expect her to trip and fall flat on her face, but she doesn't. When she is on stage she announces her song, "Oh, What a Beautiful Morning," and Ms. Dersh plays a brief introduction. Jane begins to sing. *"Oh, what a beautiful morning . . . Oh, what a beautiful day . . ."*

She is terrible. She is not only off key, but off tempo, too. I am so embarrassed for her I want to crawl under my seat. I wonder what Mr. Vanderhoot thinks of his prized pupil now?

"Thank you, Jane," Ms. Dersh says, after one chorus.

Jane doesn't take her seat again. Instead, she walks by me and whispers, "I'm going to throw up."

I am torn between going to help her and staying for tryouts. I decide to stay. I am too angry at Jane to feel sorry for her. She made her bed, now let her lie in it, I think, and then I hate myself because that is exactly what Bitsy would say.

Next, Zeigler is called, then Wright, then Wexler.

The palms of my hands are sweating. I wipe them on my skirt. I want this part so badly. I go up on stage and announce my song. I listen as Ms. Dersh plays the introduction, then I begin to sing. *"I'm just a girl who cain't say no . . . I'm in a turrible fix . . . I always say come on let's go . . . just when I ort-a say nix . . ."* I pretend that I am in the shower, singing loud and clear. I let go and smile, actually enjoying myself, as I move around the stage acting out the part of Ado Annie. I'm good. I know it. I can feel it. I release all the energy I've got. When I finish there is silence. Then Ms. Dersh says, "Thank you, Davey," in exactly the same way she'd said, *Thank you, Jane.*

That night Jane calls. "Did I make a fool of myself?"

"Yes."

"What did Ms. Dersh say?"

"She said, *Thank you, Jane.*"

"Really . . . that's all?"

"Yes."

"And what about Mr. Vanderhoot . . . what did he say?"

"Nothing."

"God . . . I'm so embarrassed."

"You should be!"

"I thought you were my friend," Jane says.

"I am. That's why I'm telling you."

Two days later the parts are posted. Jane and I go to the board outside the music center together. She sees my name before I do. "Oh, Davey . . . you got it!"

I can't believe it. I stare at my name. It's true. I got the part. "Congratulations!" I hear, over and over again. I don't even know the kids who are congratulating me.

Jane didn't even make the chorus. Neither of us is surprised.

When I get home from school Jason is in the kitchen with Bitsy, decorating cookies. "I got the part. I made it! I'm Ado Annie."

"Davey . . . that's just wonderful," Bitsy says.

I pick up Jason and dance across the room with him, singing "I Cain't Say No."

"Help . . . put me down . . ." Jason hollers.

I put Jason down and grab a carrot.

"You got a letter," Jason says.

"Where?"

"On the table."

It is a long white envelope. I hope it is from Wolf, but it's not. It's a greeting card. Outside there is a picture of Snoopy, looking forlorn. Inside it says, *Missing you, Valentine. Love, Hugh.*

I have forgotten that today is Valentine's Day. I should have known—the cookies Jason is decorating are heart shaped.

I shove the Valentine inside my notebook. It is the first time I have heard from Hugh since September, when he wrote a short letter.

"Is Mom home yet?" I ask Bitsy.

"She's upstairs, showering. Ned's coming over for dinner."

"Again?" I say, but I don't wait for her to comment. I run upstairs and knock on Mom's door. "I got the part!" I call.

Mom opens the door. She is wearing her old terry robe and drying her hair with a towel.

"What part?" she says.

I can't believe this. "In *Oklahoma!*"

"Oh, honey . . . that's wonderful."

"You know how much I wanted it, don't you?"

"Yes, of course. I thought you were talking about something else for a minute."

She takes off the robe, tosses it onto the bed and begins to get dressed.

"Why are you wearing that?" I ask, as she pulls on her best shirt. It is teal blue silk and she saves it for special occasions. She wore it last year when she and Daddy celebrated their anniversary.

"I just feel like it," Mom says. "We're having company for dinner."

"Who besides Ned?"

"No one."

"I don't consider *him* company. He's around all the time. I figure Bitsy is about to adopt him, too."

"What are you talking about?"

"You know what I mean. Add him to her collection."

"What collection?"

"Us. Jason, you, me . . . and now Ned."

"Be reasonable, Davey."

"I'm not the one who's being unreasonable, Mom."

Before dinner Jason gives me a Valentine and I feel badly that I don't have one for him.

"Open it," he says.

I open it and pull out a card made of red colored paper and a doily.

Roses are red
Violets are blue
I am your brother
And you are mine, too.

"I'm your sister, stupid!" I say, laughing.

"I know," Jason says, "but my teacher doesn't. She thinks you're a boy. You have a boy's name."

I hug him. "You're a real character . . . you know that."

"Watch it," he says, "or Count Dracula might bite your neck."

"Oh, yeah? Well, Count Dracula better watch it himself or I'll bite him back."

During dinner Mom tells The Nerd that I got a part in *Oklahoma!* He says that's terrific and that he was once in the chorus of his high school play. When he smiles I see that he has a piece of lettuce caught in his teeth.

After dinner Bitsy and Walter leave for their weekly Bridge game and Jason and The Nerd sit at the dining room table working on a model airplane.

At nine, Mom tells Jason that it's time to go upstairs. "Just a few more minutes," Jason begs.

"It's already half an hour past your bedtime," Mom says.

"Oh, all right," Jason says. "But I want Ned to carry me up . . ."

Ned scoops up Jason and throws him over his shoulder, upside down. Jason shrieks. I watch from the floor, where my books are spread out in front of me. I hate seeing Jason acting so chummy with The Nerd.

"Night, Mom . . . night, Davey . . . night, Minka . . ." Jason calls.

"Goodnight . . . sleep tight," Mom answers.

I try to concentrate on the paper I am supposed to be writing for American Cultures, but I feel Mom looking at me. There is a lot of tension between us tonight.

"He has two children of his own," Mom says quietly. "He misses them."

"Whoop-dee-doo," I say.

"Do you have to be so tough on him, Davey?"

"Who's being tough?"

Ned comes back downstairs, whistling, and settles next to Mom on the sofa.

"Would you like a brandy?" Mom asks him.

"Brandy would be nice."

Mom goes to the kitchen.

The Nerd smiles at me.

"You've got a piece of lettuce caught between your teeth," I tell him.

He turns red. I have made him uncomfortable and I am glad. He picks the lettuce from his tooth, examines it, then deposits it in the glass ashtray.

Mom comes back with the brandy and two glasses. She pours each of them a small drink and they clink glasses.

I pretend to be engrossed in my school work but what I'm really thinking is, I'd like to dump the brandy over their heads and tell them how stupid and disgusting they are.

Mom says, "Why don't you work at your desk, Davey?"

"Trying to get rid of me, *Mother?*" I ask.

"No, I just think your desk is the right place to do school work. The light isn't very good in here."

"Since when are you worried about my eyes . . . or anything else?" But I gather my books together, stand up, and leave the room.

* * *

The next morning, while I am getting ready for school, Mom comes into my room. "How would you like to have a session or two with Miriam?"

"Miriam?" I say. "Your shrink?"

"Yes. She'd like to meet you."

"Since when?"

"She's always wanted to meet you. And she's easy to talk with," Mom says.

"I'll think about it," I tell Mom.

Maybe I will go to see Miriam. There are plenty of things I'd like to tell her about my mother.

THIRTY-TWO

On Friday Jane gets drunk in school again and this time she makes a scene in the hallway. She throws her books against a row of lockers, whooping and laughing, and then she tosses her purse into the air. Everything tumbles out of it and crashes to the floor. Her mirror smashes into a million pieces and a bottle of Jean Naté breaks, leaving the hallway smelling like a perfume factory. I clean it all up and help Jane outside before she gets sick.

"You have a drinking problem," I tell her.

"I can stop anytime I want to," she says.

"Like hell!"

The next day I go to see Miriam. Mom has set up an appointment for me and although I think of cancelling at the last minute, I don't. I walk over to her office during lunch period, munching on a sandwich.

Miriam turns out to be about forty. She is my height and somewhat overweight, but in a sexy way. Her shirt is unbuttoned enough so that you can tell she isn't wearing a bra and when she walks across the room her breasts jiggle. She hikes her skirt over her knees when she sits. She is wearing textured stockings and western boots. She runs her fingers through her short brown hair several times and smiles. She doesn't seem the Los Alamos type at all. I'm surprised.

"So," she says, "how do you like it here, Davey?"

"I don't."

"Why is that?"

"It's such a bore."

"Yes, it can be. But it doesn't *have* to be."

"Maybe not," I say. I feel really uncomfortable, sure that Miriam is analyzing every word.

"It's a beautiful day, isn't it?" Miriam asks.

We're going to talk about the weather? I think. What a waste of time. But I answer, "Yes, it's a very nice day."

"So, how are things at home, Davey?"

"I'm sure my mother's already told you. We're not getting along that well."

"She mentioned that there's been some tension."

"That's putting it mildly."

"What do you think is causing it?"

"She is. She's getting to be just like them."

"Like who?"

"Walter and Bitsy. My aunt and uncle."

"In what way?"

"Well, she doesn't think for herself anymore. She does whatever they tell her to do. She lets them make all the decisions. She even lets them choose her friends." I look around the office, convinced that Miriam is recording this conversation so that she can play it back for my mother.

"You understand that what's said in this room is between you and me . . . that it doesn't go any further."

I wonder how she knows what I am thinking. "You're not going to tell my mother what I say?"

"No. I'm here to help you both, not to report on either one of you."

"Oh." I sit quietly, folding, then unfolding my hands.

"What bothers you most about your mother becoming more like Walter and Bitsy?"

"They're afraid of everything."

"Like what?"

"They won't let me learn to ski, they won't let me take Driver's Ed . . . Santa Fe is dangerous, the canyon is dangerous, just breathing is dangerous!"

"You feel they're overprotective?"

"Yes, definitely."

"Did your mother used to be less protective . . . did she let you try new things before?"

"Always."

"Do you think her reluctance to let you try new things now comes from the circumstances of your father's death?"

"I don't know," I say, looking out the window. "Maybe."

"Are you afraid of anything, Davey?"

I shrug and don't answer.

Halfway through our session Miriam says, "What about Ned . . . how do you feel about him?"

"Ned?" I say, as if I have never heard the name.

"Ned . . . your mother's friend," Miriam says.

"Oh . . . you mean The Nerd."

Miriam laughs and runs her hands through her hair. "Is that what you call him?"

"Not to his face."

"I see."

"I think he's a creep," I say, "and I don't care if you tell my mother because it's true."

Miriam nods.

"My father was very handsome and he was smart, even though he never went to college. And he was funny, too. No one around here has any sense of humor. If it weren't for Jason nobody in our house would ever laugh. But my father always had us in stitches."

"You miss him."

"Yes, I miss him." I feel myself choking up and turn away.

"You're angry, aren't you?" Miriam says.

"Sometimes," I tell her.

"It's okay to feel angry," Miriam says. "As long as you admit it and try to understand it."

When my hour is up I tell Miriam about Jane and her drinking. Miriam hands me some literature and suggests that I get Jane over to the Alcohol Abuse Clinic. "There's no charge," she says. Then she asks if I will come to see her again.

"Maybe," I say. I'm still not sure that I can trust her. So I go home and write another letter to Wolf. There are six of them in the trunk now. I wonder how long it will be before the lizards run again.

THIRTY-THREE

The first orchestra rehearsal of *Oklahoma!* is held on the afternoon of my sixteenth birthday, and when I get home from school I find that Bitsy has fixed a special dinner, with my favorite foods—chicken marengo, spinach noodles and watercress salad. She has invited Jane over. I am surprised, and pleased. The Nerd is there too. He gives me a T-shirt that says, *A Woman Without a Man is Like a Fish Without a Bicycle.* He tells us that he sent away for it after seeing the ad in *MS* Magazine. I don't get it but everyone else seems to think it's funny, so I laugh along with them and thank The Nerd. Bitsy and Walter give me a digital watch. I didn't expect anything so grand and I am really touched. I kiss Bitsy on the cheek. And then I have to thank Walter. I haven't said a word to him since the night he insulted my parents and slapped me. Now I face him. "Thank you very much." I say it formally.

"You're welcome," he answers in the same tone. "Enjoy it." He doesn't look at me. I get the feeling he is as uncomfortable about that night as I am.

Mom gives me a beautiful silver and turquoise

bracelet. It is my first piece of Indian jewelry. I put it on my right wrist, since I am already wearing my new watch on my left. Jason has painted a picture for me and has written another poem. This one says,

Roses are red
Violets are blue
You are my friend
And I am yours, too.

"Is that better?" he asks.

"Yes . . . much," I tell him, giving him a hug.

"Hey . . . let go," he says. "You're squeezing my hemorrhoids."

"What hemorrhoids?" I ask, surprised.

"Ha ha," he laughs. "Fooled you, didn't I?"

Even though I am having a good time I can't help thinking that my father and I had planned a weekend trip to New York for my sixteenth birthday. He was going to take me to a Broadway play. We used to talk about it all the time. I wonder if Mom remembers.

After the dinner plates are cleared away, Bitsy turns off the lights and comes out of the kitchen carrying a seven-layer cake. It is decorated with sixteen pink roses. She and Jason must have been working on it all week. Everyone sings "Happy Birthday." I make a wish and blow out the candles.

* * *

The next afternoon a windstorm kicks up, turning the sky brown and stinging my eyes with dust. I ride to the canyon anyway, hoping that Wolf will be there, waiting for me. But there is no sign of him. And I can't find a lizard anywhere.

THIRTY-FOUR

I hope my mother doesn't bring The Nerd to the opening night of *Oklahoma!* I don't want to hurt her feelings but I can't stand the idea of him in the audience, sitting next to my family. Twice, I come close to asking her not to bring him, but at the last minute I don't. I decide it's best not to make a big thing of it and by opening night I'm glad I let it go because I am so full of excitement about the play that I don't care if he comes with her or not.

The play begins well and by the time I do my big number the audience is warmed up and there is so much applause that I do an encore. At the end of the play we all get a standing ovation.

Reuben is the first person backstage to congratulate me. "You were great!" he says. "I always thought you were shy but I guess I was wrong."

I don't tell him that a person can be shy and still do well on the stage.

"You were really great!" he says again, pumping my hand. "I mean it."

I smile and thank him and he gives me a quick kiss, near my ear. As he does I see Mom over his shoulder. She is holding a yellow rose and looking around for me. "Mom . . ." I call. "Over here . . ."

She hands the rose to me. "You were just wonderful, Davey!" She kisses my cheek and hugs me hard. "I'm so proud of you." She is close to tears.

"Come on, Mom . . ." I say. "Everyone's looking."

"Oh." She laughs, then pulls out a tissue and blows her nose.

We perform again on Friday and Saturday night, and the boy who plays Curly, the male lead, develops laryngitis. Still, we are a great success and my picture appears in *The Monitor*, the weekly newspaper.

We have a cold snap the last week in April, and a spring snowstorm dumps thirteen inches of snow on us the first week in May. But it melts in a day and then the weather turns balmy. Everyone in school is hit with spring fever and we all cut classes and go for a hike in the Jemez mountains. There are wildflowers everywhere and the sky is a deep shade of blue.

Jane hasn't mentioned the pamphlets from Miriam. Of course, I didn't tell her they were from Miriam. I just said I'd seen them around the house—that one of Bitsy's clubs was discussing the problems of teenagers. When I gave them to Jane she didn't say anything. She just put them into her notebook.

Now, as we walk through the woods I say, "Did you have a chance to look over that stuff I gave you?"

"What stuff?"

"Those pamphlets . . . on drinking."

"Why should I waste my time reading them?"

"Because you have a drinking problem."

"I told you before. I can stop any time I want to. I don't have to drink. I do it because I like it."

"Why don't you stop lying?" I ask. "Isn't it about time you faced the facts? Isn't it about time you were honest with yourself?"

"You're a good one to talk about being honest!" Jane says.

"What do you mean?"

"You told me your father died of a heart attack. You call that honest?" She walks away in a huff.

"Jane, wait . . ." I call, hurrying to catch up with her. When I do, we walk together for a while, not speaking. Finally I say, "How did you find out?"

"Your aunt told my mother. I've known for months."

"Why didn't you say something?"

"I figured you had your reasons."

"I couldn't deal with the truth," I tell her.

She stops walking, faces me, and says, "There

are things I can't deal with either. Did you ever think of that?"

"No," I tell her. "Your life seems so easy . . ."

"Well, it's not," she says.

THIRTY-FIVE

When I get home I phone Miriam's office and set up an appointment for the next day.

Miriam greets me warmly, as if I am a long-lost friend. I sit in the same chair as last time although there is a sofa and another chair in her office.

"I read about you in *The Monitor,*" she says. "I wanted to see the play but I was out of town that weekend."

"It went well," I say.

"I'm glad." She smiles at me. "Last time we were talking about your family . . ." she begins.

But I don't wait for her to finish. "I lied about my father," I say. "I told Jane he died of a heart attack."

Miriam arches her back and leans forward. "Why do you suppose you did that?"

"I know why. Because it was easier to make up a story than to tell the truth."

"Yes . . ."

"But since then I wrote to a friend and told him that my father was shot and killed."

"Did you feel better after you told him?"

"A little . . . but I didn't tell him all of it."

"Do you want to tell me?"

"Sometimes I think I do . . . that if only I could tell someone it would help . . . but other times I'm afraid . . . I'm afraid to bring it all back."

"Maybe you have to bring it all back in order to be done with it."

I feel myself tensing and I shift in my chair, unable to find a comfortable position.

"Your mother was out with Jason on the night that your father was killed . . ." Miriam says, prompting me.

"Yes."

"Where were you?"

"I was in the backyard with my boyfriend, Hugh. We were making out when we heard the gunshots. I thought they were firecrackers."

"And then . . ." Miriam says.

"We ran to the store. I remember the sound of my screams when I saw my father on the floor. He was still alive. He said, *Help me . . . help me, Davey.* And I said, *I will . . . I will, Daddy.* I held him in my arms while Hugh phoned for help." My voice is growing smaller and smaller. Maybe I shouldn't have come back here.

"Can you go on, Davey?" Miriam asks, gently. "We'll stop if it becomes too difficult."

I feel as if the real me is very far away. Not in this room at all. When I speak my voice is barely a whisper. "I don't know how long it took before the police and the ambulance got there. I heard the sirens from a long way off. And then the flashing lights made a pattern on the walls and ceiling of the store. By then, my father was unconscious. I didn't want to let go of him. The police had to pry me loose. They let me ride to the hospital in the ambulance with him. But when we got there, Daddy was already dead."

The room is very quiet. The only sound is of an occasional car passing outside.

Finally Miriam says, "So that's how it was."

And I say, "Yes."

Then she looks away for a long time and I'm glad.

When she faces me again she says, "It must have been terribly hard to hear your father asking for help, Davey. But there was nothing you could do. It was out of your control."

"I wanted to help him. I wanted to help him more than anything." I cover my face with my hands and begin to cry.

"Of course you did," Miriam says. She hands me a box of Kleenex. "I know how it hurts."

When our session is over Miriam walks to the door with me. She puts her hand on my shoulder and squeezes it lightly. "You're beginning to deal with it, Davey, and that's important."

I step outside. My head is pounding. Just as Miriam is about to close the door I say, "I still didn't tell you all of it. I didn't tell you anything about the blood . . ." And I turn and run.

I run all the way home and go straight upstairs, to my room. I open the door to my closet, look up to the corner of the top shelf, then quickly close the door again. *I can't. I can't do it.* I sit down on the edge of my bed. My heart is beating faster and faster and I am sweating. *I have to,* I tell myself. *I have to do it.* I stand up and go back to the closet, flinging the door open, and this time, before I have a chance to think about it, I reach up and take the brown paper bag off the shelf. I grab the breadknife from the trunk, shove it into the bag, and run downstairs.

I ride Bitsy's bicycle as fast as I can, to the canyon.

I have trouble climbing down. I trip and slide several times. When I finally reach the bottom I walk directly to the cave, the cave that Wolf showed to me. I open the brown paper bag and pull out the clothes that are inside. My jeans and my halter. The clothes I was wearing that night. They are covered with dried blood and they smell terrible, but I don't care. It is my father's blood, I think. My father's blood. I hold them close for a moment, remembering.

There was blood everywhere that night. Everywhere. *It was splattered on the loaves of bread that were stacked under the cash register. It was dripping down the charcoal portrait on my father's easel. It was forming a puddle on the floor, next to my father's body. It had soaked through his clothes. And when I held him in my arms, it soaked mine, too.*

I fold the jeans and the halter and place them inside the cave, tucking the breadknife between them. I build a pyramid of rocks over them, until there is nothing left to see. Nothing but rocks.

Goodbye, Daddy. I love you. I'll always love you. This doesn't mean that I'm not going to think about you anymore. This doesn't mean that I'm never going to think about that night, either. Because that night happened. And there's nothing I can do to change the facts. But from now on I'm going to remember the good times. From now on I'm going to remember you full of life and full of love.

I sit outside the cave for a while, letting the sun warm me. Then I get up and walk away. As I do, I see a lizard racing behind a rock.

THIRTY-SIX

Two days later a small package arrives for me. There is no return address. I try to make out the postmark. I think it says Big Sur, California. I open the package quickly. Inside there is a white box and inside that, a flat, polished stone, as big as a quarter. Its colors change from brown to golden, depending on the light. It is beautiful. When I lift the stone out of the box I find a note under it. *A tiger's eye for my Tiger Eyes. Wolf.*

Where are you? I say to myself. *Los lagartijos corren. When will you be back?*

But even as I wonder I know that what matters most is that he is thinking of me, and he must know that I am thinking of him, too. I hold the tiger's eye stone to my lips.

When Mom gets home from work she says, "I've made a dinner reservation at Philomena's."

"For all of us?" I ask.

"No . . . just the two of us."

"You and me?" I say.

"Yes."

"Without Ned?"

"Yes."

"Should I change . . . should I wear a skirt?"

"If you feel like it," Mom says.

"I think I will," I tell her.

I take a shower, wash my hair and put on a gauzy blouse with my tiered skirt. I carry the stone in my pocket.

We borrow Bitsy's Volvo and drive down to Philomena's, which is the only decent restaurant in town. It is near the Los Alamos airport. We park in the lot, and as we walk across it I look up at the spring sky and see Leo.

The restaurant has a glass roof and all of the tables are shaded by yellow umbrellas. I suppose that during the day, with the sun pouring in, it makes sense, but at night, it feels funny to sit at an umbrella table.

We order green chili enchiladas and a pitcher of Sangria, which is wine that tastes like fruit punch. I like the slices of oranges and apples, floating on top.

"This is nice," I say. What I mean is that it is nice to be alone with my mother. This is the first time since we came to Los Alamos that it is just the two of us.

"Yes," Mom says. "It's very nice."

"It's been a long time."

"Yes," Mom says. "And I've wanted to explain that to you, Davey." She is arranging and re-arranging her silverware, moving the spoon into the fork's place, then the fork into the spoon's.

"Up until now, I've been afraid to be alone with you."

"Afraid?"

"Yes."

"But why?"

"I was afraid you'd ask me questions and I wouldn't have any answers. I've been afraid you'd want to talk about Daddy . . . and the night he was killed . . . and the pain would be too much for me."

"I did want to talk about it," I tell her. "For a long time . . . and it hurt me that you wouldn't."

"I know," she says, reaching across the table and touching my hand. "But I had to come to terms with it myself, first. Now I think I'm ready . . . now I can talk about it with you."

"But now I don't need to," I say.

The waitress brings our enchiladas. I take a bite and the green chili burns my mouth. "I had to deal with it too," I tell Mom. "In my own way."

Mom nods. "I guess we all did . . . in our own ways."

My mouth is on fire, and I pour myself another glass of Sangria. I think about Jane and wonder how she's doing. She would probably guzzle down the whole pitcher in five minutes. I hope she's reading the pamphlets that Miriam gave me for her.

"Ned has asked me to marry him," Mom says quietly, not looking up from her food.

I feel as if a bomb has been dropped in my lap. I can't swallow.

"But I've said *no* . . ."

I am so relieved I pour honey all over my plate instead of into the sopapilla I am holding.

"It's much too soon," Mom says. "I like him, but I don't love him."

"He can't compare to Daddy!" I tell her.

"No one is going to compare to Daddy . . . but Daddy is dead . . . and he's not coming back."

"I know that."

"Yes," Mom says. "I guess you do."

The waitress clears away our plates and asks if we'd like dessert.

"Want to share a bread pudding?" Mom asks.

"Okay." I can't help thinking about the way we are talking about my father in one breath, and in the next, we are ordering a bread pudding to share.

"When are we going home, Mom?" I hold my breath, afraid that she will say *we're never going home, Davey.*

Instead she says, "I've been thinking about it . . . I've been thinking we should leave as soon as school is over. What do you think?"

What do I think? I am overjoyed! "I can't wait," I say. "I can't wait to go home!"

"We'll have to sell the house and store.

There's no way I could go back there and besides, we'll need whatever money we can get for it."

"That's okay. Maybe we can get an apartment near the beach."

"Yes, that's what I've been thinking. And I'll have to find a job. I've written to Audrey and she thinks she might be able to help me land something in one of the hotels. I've got some credentials now. Maybe I can get into office management."

"What about Jason? Have you told him yet?"

"No, I wanted to talk to you first."

"And Walter and Bitsy?"

"Not yet."

"What do you think they'll say?"

"I think Bitsy will be terribly disappointed. She's always wanted a family and now that she's got one it's going to be hard for her to give us up."

I nod. "But Walter will be glad."

"I doubt that. He's become attached to us, too."

"Not to me."

"Even to you, Davey. It's just that he's a very rigid person . . . he only sees things his way."

"I'm glad you're not afraid anymore, Mom."

"Who says I'm not afraid?"

"You don't seem afraid tonight."

"Let me tell you something, honey . . . I used you as an excuse to come out here, and then, as an excuse to stay. I kept telling myself it was better for you and Jason, but it was really better for me. Because I was so afraid. I was running away . . . running away from the truth . . . running away from responsibilities."

"Did Miriam tell you that?"

"No . . . but it's what I learned through my sessions with her."

"She's nice. I like her."

"I thought you would."

"Daddy was never afraid of anything, was he?"

"Not true, Davey. He was afraid to take a chance on his talent. Afraid to give up the store and open a gallery. Afraid of not being a good enough husband and father. He was human. And you've got to remember that."

"I miss him a lot."

"I know. So do I."

"But I think I'm ready to get on with my life. I think that's what he'd want me to do."

Mom smiles. It is a sad smile and there are tears in her eyes.

I reach into my pocket and touch the stone.

"Hey . . . you're eating up all the bread pudding," I say.

Mom looks down at the empty dish and we both laugh.

THIRTY-SEVEN

On Sunday afternoon Mom and I go for a walk with Jason and Mom tells him that we are going home. He is full of questions. Will Walter and Bitsy come with us? What about Minka? What about Ned? What about school? What if somebody tries to kill us?

"Nobody is going to kill us," Mom tells him.

"But what if they do?"

"They won't."

"Atlantic City isn't safe. This is the only safe place," Jason says.

"That's not true." Mom is firm.

"Well, what about my cookies?"

"You can bake cookies in Atlantic City," Mom says.

"But who will help me?"

"I will," I tell him.

"You?" he says, as if that is the dumbest thing he has ever heard. "You don't know how to bake anything."

"I can learn," I tell him.

"Really?" he asks.

"Yes, really."

* * *

For the rest of the day I get the feeling that now that Jason knows we're going home he is preparing himself. He seems to be drawing closer to Mom and to me, and pulling back from Walter and Bitsy. Little kids are amazing. They seem able to adjust to anything.

I can tell that Mom is dreading telling Bitsy and Walter. She has decided to do it right after supper. Bitsy has a new pasta maker and she is cranking out whole wheat spaghetti. The sauce has been simmering all day, filling the house with a wonderful aroma, making me feel hungry long before supper time.

While we are waiting to be called to the table, Jason asks me to read him a chapter from *Charlotte's Web.* At the dinner table, he asks to sit between Mom and me. Walter looks as though he knows something is up.

After dinner, while Bitsy is sipping her second cup of coffee, Mom tells Jason he can go outside to play. As soon as he is gone she says, "I have something important to tell you."

Walter and Bitsy exchange knowing looks. Then Walter says, "I want you to know that we think Ned Grodzinski is one of the finest men we've ever met."

Bitsy smiles.

"No . . ." Mom says, realizing that they have it all wrong. "This has nothing to do with Ned. This is about us . . . Davey and Jason and me."

Now Walter and Bitsy look at each other as if

to say. *Do you know what this is all about? No, do you?*

"I'll never be able to thank you enough for all you've done . . ." Mom begins.

I really feel for her. I'd hate to be the one to have to break the news to Bitsy. I wish she'd just say it quickly and get it over with.

"What are you talking about, Gwen?" Bitsy asks.

"It's time for us to leave," Mom says. "It's time for us to start making a life on our own. We're going home. We're going home to Atlantic City."

"No!" Bitsy says.

"When?" Walter asks.

"As soon as school is over."

"But that's just a few weeks away," Bitsy says.

"Yes," Mom says. "I know."

There is an uncomfortable silence at the table. I can't look directly at either Walter or Bitsy. I fool around with the crumbs that are on my plate.

"What about the children?" Bitsy says. "They're secure here. You can't keep moving them around."

"I'm not going to," Mom says. "I'm taking them home."

"But Atlantic City . . . it's not safe . . . you, of all people should realize that, Gwen."

"I can't let safety and security become the focus of my life," Mom says.

I can't believe how sure of herself my mother sounds. I want to stand up and cheer for her.

"I thought we'd done everything to make you want to stay," Bitsy says.

"You did," Mom tells her. "You've been wonderful. Both of you. I doubt that I could have managed without you. But now . . ."

"If you want to be on your own we could help you find a place here . . . in Los Alamos . . . and you could get a permanent job at the Lab . . . and the children wouldn't have to change schools again. We have the best schools . . . everyone says so . . ." Bitsy chokes up and I realize this is going to be harder than I'd imagined.

"I can't stay," Mom says. "Please understand. I have to go home." She is on the verge of tears, too. The calm, sure voice is gone.

Bitsy stands up. "I think you're being selfish and unfair," she says, raising her voice. Then she turns and runs out of the room.

No one speaks for a long time. Finally Walter says, "She doesn't want to lose you."

"Yes, I know," Mom answers.

THIRTY-EIGHT

I ride Bitsy's bicycle to the canyon for the last time. In the bike bag is the stack of letters I have written to Wolf.

I climb down slowly, taking in the beauty of the canyon, knowing that I won't be back for a long time. That I may never come back. I want to remember the canyon exactly as it looks today. It is the place where I have felt closest to my father.

At the bottom there are lizards scurrying around. I sit on a rock and watch, turning the tiger's eye over in my hand. After a while I put the stone back into my pocket, get up, and walk to the cave. I place the letters inside, next to the pile of rocks that are covering my clothes. I have written *For Wolf Only* across the top envelope. I want him to open that one first, because inside is my note thanking him for the tiger's eye. I'm sure he will come back one day and find my letters, and when he does, he will understand. I feel certain that we will see each other again. It just won't be today.

THIRTY-NINE

"This looks like a good buy," Walter says to Mom, examining a car on Lemon Lot. Anyone who wants to sell a car in Los Alamos parks it here and potential buyers come to see what's available.

"The engine's clean, the tires are in good shape, and it will be good on gas," Walter says.

"I like the color," Mom says. "And the inside is attractive, too. What do you think, Davey?"

"I like it," I say. It is a blue Subaru and I wonder if it is the car that Jane threw up on the night we went out with Reuben and Ted.

"What do you think, Jase?"

"Is it four or five speed?" Jason asks as if he knows everything there is to know about cars.

"Five," Walter tells him.

"That'll be better for highway driving. Right, Uncle Walter?"

"Right," Walter says, tousling Jason's hair.

"Should I make them an offer?" Mom asks.

"Let's go home, call them, and set up an appointment to take it for a drive," Walter says.

"Okay . . . fine," Mom says. "And Walter . . . I really appreciate your help."

Walter nods and begins to walk toward the Blazer with Mom. Jason runs in front of them, and I hang behind.

"It's not us, is it Gwen?" Walter asks. He doesn't know I am listening.

"No," Mom says.

"Because I've been thinking about it and maybe I came on too strong."

"You were strong when I needed you to be strong," Mom says. "When I couldn't be strong myself."

"We're going to miss you and the kids," he says.

"Maybe you'll come to Atlantic City for a visit," Mom says.

Walter doesn't answer.

Jane comes over on the morning we are leaving and watches as I pack. "I don't know what I'm going to do without you, Davey," she says. She is crying. She's been crying ever since she got to our house.

"You'll be okay." I try to reassure her. But I don't really believe it. She has admitted that she has a drinking problem. She took a test in one of those pamphlets I gave her and the results proved that she has alcoholic tendencies and might actually be an alcoholic. Now it is up to her to go to the Alcohol Abuse Clinic and get help. I set up two appointments for her last week but she freaked out and didn't keep either of them. "You're getting too dependent on me," I tell her. "It's good that I'm leaving. It's really unhealthy when you get too dependent on someone else. Believe me . . . I know . . ."

"But you're my only friend," she cries, "and I'm never going to see you again."

"Sure you will," I say. "You'll come to Atlantic City for a visit. It's about time you saw the ocean." I laugh, trying to cheer her up, but it's no use.

"I'm never going to see anything," she says. "I'm going to spend the rest of my life here, in Los Alamos, just like my sister. I know it."

"You don't have to if you don't want to."

"I don't want to . . . but I'm scared not to."

"You've got to stop being scared."

"That's easy for you to say."

"No, it's not."

"I'm sorry . . . I didn't mean . . ."

"It's okay. Forget it."

"Davey . . ." Bitsy calls. "Are you almost ready?"

"In a minute," I call back.

Jane and I hug each other. "I'm glad we got to be friends," I tell her.

"Will you always be my friend?" she asks.

"Yes," I say. "Always."

I am throwing some last minute things into my knapsack when Bitsy comes to my room.

"Your mother's waiting for you, Davey."

"I'm ready," I say. Minka is sitting on my bed wondering what's going on. I pick her up and look around my room. It looks the way it did on the day I came here.

"I don't know what Gwen's trying to prove," Bitsy says. "I don't know why she thinks she has to do this."

"La vida es una buena aventura," I say, pleased with myself. I have picked up several Spanish phrases and this is one of them.

"What does that mean?" Bitsy asks.

"It means that life is a good adventure."

Bitsy hugs me. "Sometimes it is and sometimes it isn't," she says. "I'm going to miss you, Davey. I'm going to miss all of you."

I pat Bitsy on the back.

"And I'll be so worried about you."

"You don't have to worry, Aunt Bitsy. We're going to be all right."

FORTY

Jason races down the beach, his Dracula cape flying behind him. Mom and I are quiet, listening to the sound of the surf crashing against the jetty.

There are so many memories here in Atlantic City. But you can't go back. Not ever. You have to pick up the pieces and keep moving ahead.

I think about Lenaya and Hugh. Will they know how much I've changed this year? Will they have changed too? I'll wait until tomorrow to find out. And then it's possible I won't find out after all. Because some changes happen deep down inside of you. And the truth is, only you know about them. Maybe that's the way it's supposed to be.

Judy Blume talks about writing Tiger Eyes

Although there's a violent crime at the center of the story, *Tiger Eyes* isn't about violence. It's about the sudden, tragic loss of someone you love. I lost my beloved father suddenly, when I was twenty-one. He died, not as the result of a violent crime, but of a heart attack at home. I was with him. I still can't write this without choking up, remembering. Davey's feelings about her father's sudden death were based on mine, though I'm not sure I was aware of it while I was writing the book.

I lived in Los Alamos, New Mexico, the setting of the book, for two years. My teenage children went to school there. It wasn't a happy experience, but it helped me write what George (my husband) and Larry (my grown son) think is my best book. It allowed me to write about a world I would never have known, about characters I'd never have imagined. Yet I had no idea, while I was living there, that I would ever write a book set in that town. All I could think of was getting out. It took a few years to look back and see it more clearly.